FROM THE WILLOWS: THE CURSE OF THE DARK MOON

From the Willows: The Curse of the Dark Moon

Eli James Smock

Contents

ISBN: 979-8-218-45755-6 (Paperback)

ISBN: 979-8-218-45756-3 (Ebook)

Library of Congress Control Number: 2024915986

This is a work of fiction. Names, characters, places, and incidents are either the product of the author's imagination or used fictitiously, and any resemblance to actual persons, living or dead, business establishments, events, or locales is entirely coincidental.

Printed in the U.S.A.
Hingham, MA

First Printing, 2024

One

Beagle and Bengal

Dark, billowing snow clouds stained the gray mountain sky. A storm had struck the massive, ancient mountain range known as the Enlightened Mountains. Though this range was no stranger to intense weather, it had seen nothing like this monster in the darkest of winters, and it was now early spring. Temperatures far below freezing combined with harsh winds to make a force powerful enough to wipe out a village, if anyone would dare to try and make a civilization up on these desolate peaks.

All that said, not many people visited the Enlightened Mountains. Quite frankly, the majority of the population was unaware of its existence. Those who did know about it chose to stay away from it, as it was one of the most dangerous mountain ranges in Alaska, maybe even in the world! Frigid temperatures, grizzly bears, wolves, lack of oxygen from the high altitude, and many more dangers (not to mention the deadly storm that currently wreaked havoc through the peaks) convinced people to stay away.

But there was one person who lived there, residing in a cave high in the peaks of these dangerous mountains. And this man was no ordinary person.

He lived alone, besides his two faithful pets. They were as un-ordinary as the man himself (if not more, of course), for rather than hiding deep in their cave to escape the temperatures as the man currently did, they were out braving their ways through the swirling white storm. As they finished their tasks, they began to travel back towards the cave, not to escape the cold, but to deliver highly important information to the man. In fact, it was information that could determine the fate of the entire world. So, the pets traveled with much haste regardless of the storm.

Around midday, a highly strange occurrence took place just outside of the man's cave (which lay on top of the tallest peak in the range); a small cloud seemed to descend in elevation from the others, lowering itself towards the mouth of the cave. This cloud simply did not seem to fit in with the others, not only due to its strange behavior but also because of its odd appearance; for one thing, it was a bright, pearly white, unlike the other dark gray storm clouds. And, for another thing, it was shaped like the head of a beagle!

The strangely shaped cloud let out a yip of pleasure (such as a dog might do) and stared down at the cave. It tilted its head so it pointed right towards the entrance. Then, the beagle cloud spat out a burst of lightning from its mouth that rocketed down right to the entrance of the vast mountainous cavern... and continued to strike as if a wire flowed from the cloud's mouth to the cave's opening! Slowly, as the lightning ray continued to zap the same spot, the cloud began to disappear, and, much more strangely, a real live beagle began to form in the spot the lightning struck! When the lightning stopped, and the cloud was gone, a brown spotted beagle with wide, round eyes stood at the entrance of the cave. It let out its same yip, and this time, a voice from within the cave responded.

"I'm coming, Watt," shivered a tired and slightly distraught voice. The man must have been very deep inside the cave, as the beagle named Watt could only hear the bleak echo of the familiar voice of his master.

While the beagle was waiting for the man, he shivered and stared out into the distance; though the colossal amounts of falling snow obscured much of the gray landscape, he could make out icy pine trees among the mountaintops. But, in the distance, he also noticed another strange phenomenon running towards him. Paw prints began appearing in the deep snow, rapidly growing closer. The invisible being making them must have been going at least thirty miles an hour! They skittered and scattered and leaped and jumped, climbing higher and higher up the dark rocky mountainside with immense speed and agility. The thing that made them had to have been quite agile and quick to have leaped up the mountain so quickly, especially in the massive storm. Closer and closer to the beagle it came, leaping from ledge to ledge, higher and higher...

Then, before the little beagle knew it, the invisible creature leaped up from a point just below the opening of the cave and stopped right in front of him, and paw prints formed directly in front of the poor shivering beagle. They lingered for a moment, but then, an animal faded into view with its feet in the paw prints. It was a large and beautiful Bengal cat, with wide, blue eyes.

"Ah, Fade, you're here too," the voice said again. It was arriving closer to the mouth of the cave, echoing footsteps growing louder and louder. Fade (the Bengal) meowed, and Watt (the beagle) made his yipping noise. Then, a man emerged from the cave.

He was wearing a ragged brown robe, such as an old wizard might wear (though he was quite young), and underneath, baggy pants that fell to the ground and a collared, blue checkered shirt (although this was barely visible because of the robe). He held a tall wooden staff (taller than he was) that was slightly twisted and gnarled, like an old vine. On the tip of his staff was a lumpy magenta crystal, shimmering brightly despite the dark clouds. He couldn't have been a day older than thirty, with short, black, curly hair. His face looked very tired, and he had bags under his eyes due to lack of sleep. This man was Hermes Willowlands.

"So," he said, as he clapped his hands, rubbing them together, and looked at his two magical pets. He seemed to barely notice the ghastly weather surrounding him, though his robe flapped violently in the breeze. "I'm assuming you have news for me?" Watt and Fade nodded and made synchronized yipping and meowing noises.

"Whoa, whoa, hold your horses," he said, smiling. He raised his staff and tapped the crystal on his head. A ghostly magenta ripple echoed through his body, and he said, "Alright, now tell me what's going on."

Watt and Fade yipped and meowed again, but because of the magical ripple-like spell he had cast on himself, Hermes heard something different. He was used to casting these Interpretation Spells to communicate with his two pets; after all, he had been sending them on scouting missions for years to obtain information. However, the information Watt and Fade delivered to him was not something he would receive every day. They didn't say much, but it was enough. Enough to jog back horrible memories, forgotten years, and one of the worst experiences of his life. What Watt and Fade said to him in unison was enough to make the most peaceful person stressed and anxious, the strongest person weak, and the happiest person suddenly depressed and defeated. "Odious," the pets said.

Hermes turned as pale as a crisp piece of paper, and it wasn't because of the cold. "So the rumors you have been reporting to me for the last few weeks have been true," he said, muttering to himself. "She is to return…"

The pets nodded but with very sorrowful looks on their faces.

"Then we must warn everyone in the area," Hermes declared, trying as hard as he could to sound brave. Then he turned to his pets and explained, "You know, the place where he banished her."

The pets nodded and began yipping and meowing again. But Hermes did not know what they were saying, because his spell was wearing off. Maybe if he had known, he wouldn't have sent Watt and Fade down to evacuate the inhabitants. Maybe if he had known, the events following wouldn't have happened. "Odious escaped," they said in unison, "from the prison in Metronome Woodland."

But Hermes did not hear. "Go to the town, and get everyone out," he commanded, "and that means everyone."

The pets bowed their heads. Hermes had not heard their warning. But they could not disobey a direct order. The young man retreated back into the depths of the cave, shuddering slightly now, and Watt and Fade turned back to the treacherous conditions that awaited their travel. Suddenly, a lightning bolt struck Watt directly in the head, and after a few minutes, the pearly white beagle-head cloud appeared once more in the sky. At the same time, Fade seemed to disappear from existence until all that was left were her four paw prints sitting in the snow. Then, they began their trek down the Enlightened Mountains all the way to a certain nearby Alaskan village.

Fade twisted and turned, jumping over rocks and prancing beside the frozen rivers, now and then glancing at Watt flying above, darting over and under the massive gray storm clouds. They passed snow-covered forests, boulders, and even a humongous frozen lake that Fade skittered across, her claws making mysterious scrape marks on the ice. As they journeyed on, the storm began to die down, for it had already passed through this area days before. The clouds thinned out until none remained, revealing the starry sky.

With the sky free, Watt stared down until he spotted the tiny, distant village. He signaled to Fade, and together, they plummeted towards it. They finally reached their destination at around three in the morning and stopped right in the center of the slush-covered village.

It was so small, Watt and Fade weren't sure if they'd even call it a village. There were only about twenty little homes in the area, each of them looking like something out of a fairy tale.

The tall wooden houses stood motionlessly on the snow-covered streets. Each had small windows coated in frost, and beautiful doors in shades of white, blue, red, and green, each completed with a shimmering bright doorknob.

The nearest school was a few miles away, in another chilly Alaskan town, so the main inhabitants of the tiny village were either extremely old or young men and women who had no children and enjoyed hiking in the wilderness.

The pets patrolled the streets, looking into the windows of the houses. After their search, they found that the vast majority of the houses were empty. The gargantuan snowstorm that had just blown through the tiny town scared much of the tiny village's population, making them book flights to places nearer to the equator. But the storm was over, and the villagers hadn't returned. Even the townsfolk that had braved the terrible storm had gone away for Spring Break, off to visit family members or ski before the summer weather came in. At least, most of them had gone away.

Sixteen of the houses appeared to be vacated but regularly maintained. Two of them appeared to be for sale. One of them was run down, and it looked like no one had been in it for years. Only one house appeared to have people currently residing in it. It was a tall, blue house with a majestic green willow tree of monstrous proportions stationed outside.

Inside this house lived the Evans family. Mr. and Mrs. Evans both worked for the Purple Mountain Journal (named after the nearby and very majestic mountain range, the Purple Mountains), a local newspaper. Their son, Teddy Evans, was twelve. However, they were not the only ones staying in this beautiful blue house. Visiting for Spring Break were Mrs. Evans's sister and husband, Mrs. and Mr. Robinson, and Mr. Evans's brother and wife, Mr. and Mrs. Monty. The Robinsons' daughter Wendy was sixteen, and the Montys' son Justin was fourteen. All of the parents were great friends and visited each other often. The Evanses and the Montys had visited the Robinson household for Christmas break in their house in California. The Robinsons and the Evanses had visited the Monty's home in New York during winter break. And now, it was time for the Evanses to host (much to Teddy's displeasure).

Watt turned himself back into a beagle in a zap of lightning, and Fade appeared in the middle of the street. Both animals peered into the window of the topmost bedroom. Suddenly, they saw movement and hid behind the mammoth willow tree.

Inside the house, nearly everybody was fast asleep. Everyone was dreaming peacefully, thoughts of other matters on their minds rather than the beagle and the Bengal outside. Everyone except for one boy. And that boy was Teddy Evans.

Two

The House Beside the Willow

Teddy Evans had been tossing and turning for hours. Teddy was a scraggly boy with short (but messy) light brown hair and an assortment of freckles. He glanced around his room and groaned; on the floor next to his bed were his cousins Wendy and Justin on air mattresses. He asked himself, why did they have to stay for a whole week? Wendy was overprotective of him, worse than his mom, and Justin considered a day wasted if he hadn't made fun of Teddy at least thrice. The true reason Teddy lay awake in his bed restlessly was because he dreaded the day that followed. In his opinion, every day with Justin and Wendy was a day he could never get back.

Teddy sighed internally. The worst part of his cousins coming over was the fighting. Justin and Wendy got along with each other fine, apart from the occasional disagreement, but neither seemed to like him much. It seemed like they'd been picking on him since the moment they met. Teddy remembered angrily when they had first met. At the time, he was in first grade, and Justin bet him fifteen dollars that Teddy couldn't climb up the house and back without falling. Teddy happened to be very skilled at climbing (even at a young age) and had made it to the roof when Wendy saw him, climbed up herself, and carried him down. She had yelled at him for what seemed like hours, and as if that wasn't enough, she told Mrs. Evans who grounded him and forbade him from going outside unattended for a month. Even after that, Justin wouldn't give him his fifteen dollars because technically, Wendy had carried him down.

He was infuriated by even the thought of this memory, and he thought of it often, which was why he always despised the visits from Justin and Wendy.

He sat up and looked around his yard, searching for any possible way he could get away from the torment of his cousins for a whole week.

All of a sudden, he saw a flash of movement: two animals that couldn't have been taller than his knees. He blinked and looked again, only to find they had disappeared from view. He began unlatching the window to try to see better when he heard his cousins stir.

"Teddy, you woke me up," Wendy complained sleepily and she put on her glasses. She had long, black, curly hair. Her hazel eyes glared annoyedly at Teddy.

Justin sat up and stared at him unlatching the window. "What are you trying to do, run away?" he sneered. Justin was a handsome boy but almost always had a nasty grin on his pointed face.

He had long and messy blonde hair, which made him look like he had bed-head even in the middle of the day. Teddy scowled at his cousins and they both laid down and went back to sleep.

He snuck a glance out the window; still nothing. Then he looked at his clock and yawned. He would look for the creatures the next day… Now, he needed sleep…

However, although Teddy didn't hear it, Watt and Fade prowled around his house all night, searching for ways in. They checked for unlocked windows and doors, and by the time everyone in the Evans house was awake, they were ready to begin the evacuation of the people of the small Alaskan village.

By eight o'clock in the morning, everyone was awake. Everyone had changed out of their pajamas and into their normal clothing. Teddy wore a T-shirt and jeans. Justin put on a purple shirt covered by his usual green vest. Wendy wore her usual orange sweater, knitted by herself.

Meanwhile, out on the lawn, Watt and Fade had hidden behind the willow tree the night before, and now they only needed a chance for everyone to come outside. They were patient, waiting for just the right moment to surprise the family and (somehow) quickly get them out of the area.

Inside the house, spirits were alive and high. Mrs. Evans greeted the kids excitedly with a look of mixed panic and happiness as they trudged down the stairs.

"Children, children!" Mrs. Evans exclaimed, panting heavily with excitement. "This is the news story of the century!" She turned the living room TV on, and the screen lit up. "Watch!"

"A large breakout took place in a high-security prison that we're not allowed to give the name of," a bald news reporter said.

"The four escapees were the famous criminals Marco Victor Odious, Dylan McCamel, Michelle Laurens, and Shannon Jones. These criminals were involved in a burglary years ago of a very valuable crystal owned by a man named 'Hermes Willowlands'. He said the crystal was a very rare artifact, calling it 'one of a kind' and 'irreplaceable'. Police and officials highly doubted this piece of information, but they still arrested the four crooks for robbery. Hermes Willowlands was later deemed insane, as authorities found out that he was trying to stop the criminals himself rather than letting the police handle the situation. In addition to this, Willowlands disappeared the day after the crystal was recovered, never to be seen again. It is also possible that these escapees have kidnapped him, so if you see any of the four criminals, make sure to look for another man with them as well before contacting your local police station."

Images of Odious, McCamel, Laurens, and Jones were put up on the television, which wasn't very helpful, as they were wearing cloaks with their hoods covering their faces, presumably to hide their identities. A photograph of the crystal was also put up, and if Teddy hadn't known better, he would've assumed it had magical powers.

"That prison is a few miles away from our town!" Mr. Evans told them excitedly, as he ran over to his wife. "We have to go there and do a piece for the Purple Mountain Journal before those idiots from the news station broadcast the story to the whole world!"

"We could use the extra publicity," Mrs. Evans continued. "I think people are getting bored with our newspaper, so we should add more interesting topics. For example, I was thinking of an inside scoop on the fifth page of the recent ban on dead raccoons in the nearby gym after Mr. Timer brought one in after he ran it over would get people interested…"

Teddy had learned just to drown out his parents' newspaper ideas. He never wanted to admit it, but sometimes he thought that his parents cared more about publicity than about him. But as he watched Justin display a mimicry of Mr. and Mrs. Evans jabbering at high speeds in an obnoxious voice, he thought of what his cousins would say if they knew what he felt inside.

Wendy would say something that would go a little something like, "Good. Maybe now that you're so mature you'll stop causing so much trouble."

Justin would just snicker rudely and say, "You actually care about what they think about you?"

Finally, Mr. and Mrs. Evans's long talk was over, and Mr. Evans told the three cousins, "All right, we've got to go and get that story. Wendy and Justin, your parents have decided to come with us to try to learn the ropes. We may be gone overnight, so we already made you dinner. It's in the oven, so try not to burn your hands. Oh, and Teddy, don't go outside unless Wendy's supervising you."

"I can supervise myself!" Teddy complained.

"It's for your own good," Wendy said, and Mr. Evans nodded.

"Hurry up!" Mrs. Evans said impatiently to her husband. "If we don't report on this story, our newspaper may go out of business! Bye, kids."

The two of them rushed out the door. "We're coming!" Mr. Robinson called, and the rest of the parents followed the two reporters.

Teddy made himself a bowl of cereal and sank into the couch. "They're so dramatic," he muttered under his breath. He turned on a documentary on the ocean and tried to get himself absorbed in the program, away from his troubles. But then, he heard a strange clattering noise and glanced out the window and gasped; he saw what looked like the two animals he had seen the night before!

Now that he could see them more clearly, he took a good, long look; one of them was a little brown-spotted beagle, the other a blue-eyed Bengal, both looking towards the Evans parents driving away at a dangerously high speed.

The pets of Hermes Willowlands finally realized someone was watching them and quickly turned their heads toward the window. Seeing Teddy, they dashed away from the window in fear. He jumped up off the couch, spilling his cereal, and followed them through the view of the windows. Running through the house, he glanced out of every window he saw, following their movements.

Eventually, Teddy lost their location. He ran upstairs, trying to get a better view. He leaped across the hallway and threw open another window, only to once again find nothing. Then, he heard Wendy's voice call up to him.

"Teddy, another mess I have to clean up!" she yelled up the stairs with a groan; presumably, she had found his breakfast splattered across the floor. He heard her muttering under her breath from the room below about how she would never have kids.

Wendy hadn't seen him yet, so he darted to his room overlooking the gargantuan willow tree. He opened his window and looked out.

A swaying branch stood out right below his peeping face. It wasn't very high off the ground, but it was just high enough for him to break a bone if he took a slip while attempting to balance on it. He closed his eyes, held his breath, and stepped onto the rickety bough.

The branch swayed a little, bouncing up and down. Teddy didn't even realize he was holding his breath until his face turned bright red. Gasping for air, he waited until the swaying stopped, and then took another step. The branch didn't break.

Continuing to make little steps across the branch, he peeled his eyes for the beagle and the Bengal. But he forgot all about them when he reached the end of the branch.

He stood in a flat area made up of many branches that sprung out in every direction. Drooping green leaves plummeted down from above and to the sides of him, so he was hidden from view. However, he could see everything on the outside of the tree perfectly. It was like a natural tree fort!

He climbed a little higher, and eventually his head popped up right over the leaves.

Teddy began to feel a bit nervous, as the tree stretched much above his house. He assumed if there were a third story on his house, the tree would've still been taller.

As it swayed in the wind, Teddy shivered in his navy blue coat and stared down, searching for the pets as the wind whipped against his face.

Then, he heard Wendy call, "Teddy, where are you? You're my responsibility!" He heard her stomping up the stairs to his room. Then, she poked her head out his window. Teddy gulped and ducked down.

Wendy looked around, then shook her head, deciding Teddy was inside. He relaxed and continued to look for the two animals.

Many minutes passed. Teddy sighed. He stared down, hoping to catch even just a glimpse of the creatures he had seen. He thought that he maybe just had a bad viewpoint and shuffled around, but still nothing. But then, just as he was beginning to give up hope, they came into view.

They circled each other and then began yipping and meowing oddly. It appeared they were communicating in some way, even though Teddy knew that cats and dogs couldn't understand each other.

He watched them for a little longer, but it was clear that there was nothing special about them.

He laughed at his foolishness. They were probably just strays.

But then, all of a sudden, a lightning bolt shot down into the yard! Teddy nearly fell out of the tree. His face turned pale, his eyes widened, and the hairs on his head seemed to stand on end. He dove beneath the cover of one of the branches, dismayed that he was in one of the worst possible places during a lightning storm: a high tree.

But it was not a lightning storm. No strikes followed. He glanced at the ground. The animals were gone, but even more strangely, there wasn't a single singe mark on the yard, or anywhere else for that matter. Had he hallucinated? What in the world was wrong with him?

Then, he heard Wendy stomping up to his room. He quickly exited the willow tree across the rickety branch that led to his window. He jumped through, picked up a pencil, and sat at his desk with a piece of his Spring Break homework, acting like he had been there all along.

Wendy walked in and slammed the door shut. "All right," she said. "Now, you're coming down to the living room. I want to have my eye on you the whole time in case you go off and disappear again."

Teddy sighed with relief that she had not scolded him more and followed her down the stairs. Then, he decided to ask her something. "Wendy, can I go outside?"

She thought about it for a moment. "Okay, fine, but I have to be watching you the whole time..."

Teddy didn't hear the rest; he was already running down the stairs toward the front door.

Anxiously, he burst through the door to inspect the clouds. He thought, if mysterious lightning was shooting down into his yard, surely the reason lay within the clouds.

He looked at the gray cumulonimbi. They seemed to be gathered only around his house, with a blue sky surrounding the rest of the neighborhood. He had many questions. Why wasn't it raining? Why were the clouds grouped in such an odd formation? Why did a single spurt of lightning come down and cause those animals to disappear?

Sighing, he went over and started to play pass with Justin, who was kicking around a soccer ball. But in mid-kick, he noticed something about the clouds. There were only two of them. And they were shaped like the heads of the beagle and the Bengal! He blinked and looked again. What was going on?

"Justin, look at those crazy clouds!" Teddy exclaimed.

"I've got more on my mind than just a bunch of dumb clouds," Justin spat.

"No, look!"

Finally, after much more convincing, Teddy got Justin to look up... but they, like all of the other evidence that anything had happened, had disappeared! Justin looked at him funny and then went back to kicking around the soccer ball.

As a matter of fact, the two pets could share their powers. Just as Watt had assisted Fade in becoming a cloud, Fade could turn them both invisible.

While the invisible animal-head-shaped clouds floated around, Teddy sat down on the front steps. Perhaps he had fallen ill? He was seeing things, impossible things.

Justin came over to him. "What's with you today?" he asked, but not in a kind and caring way.

Wendy (who had followed Teddy outside) came over too. "Yeah, Teddy, what's going on?"

"I saw these weird animals running around, and then... I thought I saw a strike of lightning hit the ground!" he told them truthfully. Justin let out a snicker, and Wendy clucked at him disapprovingly. Teddy sighed to himself; this was exactly why he hadn't told Justin and Wendy about the creatures in the first place (even though he probably could have said it a tad more subtly).

Teddy glared up at the roof; he didn't want to look them in the eye. Couldn't they just listen and understand him for once? Sure, Teddy thought he was crazy himself, but couldn't they be a little more understanding?

Wendy and Justin followed his gaze to the roof. "What are you looking at?" Justin sneered.

Suddenly, a small chunk of the roof exploded! The three of them gasped. They thought, maybe Teddy was telling the truth after all.

Watt and Fade had just landed on the roof. Even though they were both invisible (thanks to Fade), the lightning bolt left its effects on the roof. Burn marks and a large hole proved to Teddy, Wendy, and Justin that something had happened.

The two pets looked at the three children staring at them. Though they were invisible, they knew they had been caught. The evacuation plan had failed. There was only one thing for them to do.

Fade made them visible again, and they both climbed down from the tall house. Landing in a slushy puddle, they walked over to the gaping cousins.

Teddy was the first to exit his state of shock and surprise and smirked at Wendy and Justin. They were too shocked about the duo of magical pets to notice.

Watt and Fade looked at each other and nodded. Then, Watt created a puffy cloud, and Fade turned it invisible to avoid the prying eyes of humans in other villages. Invisibly, it sped back to the cave where the sorcerer called Hermes Willowlands resided, bringing the news of the three children who had resisted the evacuation.

Three

In Metronome Woodland

Four figures crashed through the Alaskan forest known as Metronome Woodland, fueled purely by adrenaline. They had been relentlessly chased by the authorities for hours. The police were closing in, and because they had the advantage of motorized vehicles, it seemed that the fugitives would be caught. However, the bandits knew the forest well, and they used that knowledge to their advantage.

They took a shortcut through a patch of brambles and headed for the nearby swamp. The police drove around the thorn patch and followed alongside the criminals. The four cloaked figures were nimble and got through the brambles with hardly a scratch, but the cops were still gaining on them. Though they were exhausted, they knew they would be free if they entered the bog, so they crept as quietly and quickly as possible into the mucky water.

The swamp water was surprisingly deep, which played to their advantage. One by one, the criminals sank until they were laying on the dirty floor of the pond. The water rippled as they heard the officers jump out of their police cars and begin searching the swamp of gigantic proportions. The criminals knew they couldn't hold their breath too long, so they began swimming quickly through the sludge-like water. They only stopped to breathe when they knew that no one was looking their way. The journey was slow, but soon, they made it to the end of the disgusting bog, which was far away from prying eyes.

They trudged slowly without a word, hiding when they heard even the slightest noise; after all, who knew what could be hiding in that forest?

Eventually, they had come to realize they were safe, and they began running again until they reached a clearing.

The first person to break through the clearing was wearing a black cloak. Visible through his cloak were dark blue eyes and a goatee. He looked around the empty forest and scowled; though he had escaped from imprisonment, he was not free.

The next person to break through the clearing was one wearing a mustard yellow cloak. It was another man, and he lowered his hood, revealing short, sandy hair. He looked at the man in the black cloak and bowed.

Then, a person wearing a blood red cloak came charging through the trees. She lowered her hood, revealing blonde hair that trickled down her back. "Are we still being followed?" she panted. The man in the yellow cloak shook his head.

Finally, a woman in a light plum cloak joined the group. After making sure everyone was there, she too lowered her hood, revealing a smirk on her face. She had black hair held in a ponytail.

After making sure they were alone, the man in the black cloak lowered his hood. He was much older than the others, whose ages spanned from twenty-five to thirty. He was bald and had a menacing look that could silence the bravest person in the world. He looked around and scowled harder. Finally, he spoke in a grizzled voice.

"Eight years ago, you three failed me," he said bitterly. "Eight years ago, you couldn't steal what I ordered you to. Eight years ago, instead of ending up the richest, most powerful people in the world, we ended up in prison! Explain yourselves!"

He looked at each of them, one at a time. "You!" he shouted at the man in the yellow cloak. "Dylan McCamel... what happened?"

The man in the yellow cloak named Dylan McCamel trembled; he couldn't help it. "I... I don't know, sir." He trembled harder as the cloaked man glared at him. "I... I may have calculated wrong..."

"Silence!" the man in the black cloak yelled, and Dylan McCamel trembled. The man in black smiled at his intimidation skills. He moved on to the woman in the blood red cloak.

"Ah, Michelle Laurens," he said and glared harder. "Now, what did you do wrong?"

"I... I... I'm sure I didn't do anything wrong... it was mostly the others..." she started, and the cloaked man put his hands on her shoulders and shook her hard.

"Idiot," he muttered. "If you had done your job, why did we end up in jail for stealing?!

"And… you," he continued, onto the woman in the light plum cloak. "Shannon Jones."

She smiled. "Guilty as charged."

The man in black glared. "Disrespecting the rules… insulting me… I would kill you harshly if you weren't such a good thief!"

"Good thing I am, old man, or I'd surely be dead to your amazing slapping skills," she said sarcastically. She smiled a mischievous smile. Steam was practically billowing out of the man in the black cloak's ears. He scowled and drew himself up to his full height.

"Do you all know who I am?" he asked menacingly. "I am the greatest criminal in the entire world… the best of the best. I've trained the strongest scalawags in the world… Becca Foreman, Leonard Ruckson, and even the notorious Damien Komodo. But you treat me like filth. You're almost as bad as those pesky hunters I trained many years ago… they must be in their sixties by now: Vincent and Ulysses Rogers. They were better than you, but I didn't choose them to carry out the deed. Oh, no. I chose three foolish, young little riffraff. You three. Do you know why?"

The three misdemeanants had been silent for the man in black's long rant.

"No," Michelle Laurens trembled.

The man smiled. His skeletal face grew into a spooky grin. "It's because you're stupid. You know nothing of the world. You're weak. You won't murder me in my sleep and fulfill the quest yourself. Unlike the Rogers brothers."

He spat. "I've regretted my decision. You've dirtied my name, my criminal name that has been in the records for years. Do you know how that feels?"

Dylan McCamel shuddered. "No, master."

"No, master," the man in black said mockingly. "What, are you afraid to say my name?" A long silence passed.

Finally, Shannon Jones spoke up, and even though she was the least afraid of him, her mouth still trembled as she formed the words. "No, Marco Victor Odious." Dylan McCamel and Michelle Laurens quivered. The man in the black cloak was none other than one of the most famous criminals in history, Marco Victor Odious. The words seemed to pierce through the air as Shannon Jones said them, echoing all throughout Metronome Woodland.

Marco Victor Odious let out a cold, cruel laugh. "Now," he said, "do any of you riffraff know how we got out of jail?"

"Possibly because of your skill, Master… Odious?" Dylan McCamel guessed, shuddering out the last word.

Marco Victor Odious glared. "Petty, misguided fool," he spat. "You think complimenting me will make me want to destroy you less?"

Dylan McCamel nearly fainted at that. "Anyway, the reason we escaped wasn't because of me," Marco Victor Odious continued. "A close friend of mine snuck in, disguised herself as a jail guard, and then shut the power off. Then, she freed me, I burst you buffoons out, and then we exited. And, we would've been caught if she hadn't turned on the emergency lockdown inside of the jail."

"So?" Shannon Jones asked.

"So?" Marco Victor Odious repeated, snarling ferociously. "So, I've proved you three are complete idiots! You can't do anything! ANYTHING! And do you know what I do to idiots..."

He drew a blade from a hidden pocket inside his cloak. Michelle Laurens gasped. Dylan McCamel's eyes grew to the sizes of watermelons. Even Shannon Jones shuddered a bit. But then, he returned the blade to his pocket.

"The only reason I need you three is because I need some henchmen to spare," he said quietly. "You do the work, I do the ordering. Otherwise, it's a choice between me turning you into the authorities for good or annihilation. So shut up, follow the rules, and most importantly... do whatever I say. And do it right."

A cold silence followed. "Now, you all know why we got into jail in the first place," he said. "An artifact that would have let us practically rule the world if we had collected it. The Thunder Crystal."

Marco Victor Odious continued. "As you know, the Thunder Crystal has many magical capabilities, although it is not necessarily one of the stronger magical artifacts in this world. It was owned by seven different sorcerers after its famous creation by Caesar Knotweigh. Undoubtedly, the most famous possessor of this unique stone was Michael Nightwhale, one of the greatest sorcerers of the world...

"At the time Michael Nightwhale was alive, one of the most evil entities ever to roam the earth was alive, and she destroyed half of the worldwide sorcerers... the Oracle. Commanding thousands of witches, she seemed impossible to stop... until Michael Nightwhale had an idea.

"Protected in an ancient vault, there is a book. And not just any book… an exceptional book, *Magic of the Dark Moon.* This book contains the darkest, most powerful spells in the world, fueled by the power of the Dark Moon. These spells can only be achieved by a very powerful object, like the Thunder Crystal. Now, Michael Nightwhale asked for permission for one of these spells, as the spells of the Dark Moon are clearly forbidden among sorcerers worldwide.

"Everyone agreed that it had to be done, so Michael Night-whale used the Thunder Crystal to cast one of the most danger-ous curses: the Interdiction Curse. And so, the Oracle and her army of witches were sucked into the Thunder Crystal, never to be seen again.

"Now, if we free the Oracle from her prison on the night of the Dark Moon, we would share the rulership with the Oracle after she conquers the rest of the world. We could easily destroy all of the non-magical people in the world, as fewer sorcerers are alive today because of the Oracle's previous invasion. So, I hope you will not fail me this time. Because if you do, you will be making a grave mistake."

Marco Victor Odious snarled those last words and put his hood back up.

"Your task at the moment is simple… find Hermes Willow-lands and figure out his plan of action," he commanded the bandits. "Once you figure out where he's headed, report back to me. And if you see any other sorcerers, do not engage. Orion is said to roam these woods, and I do not want you dealing with that idiot."

And with that, the three bandits were off.

Four

Hermes Willowlands

It had been hours since the cloud had sped off into the mountains, and the three cousins were beginning to grow restless. It was late afternoon, and Watt and Fade hadn't let them move an inch. They knew their master would be arriving soon, and they had to be present at his arrival.

Teddy sighed, and asked, "How much longer are we going to wait out here?" Wendy and Justin looked at him and grunted in annoyance. The children had stopped asking questions in the late morning after they realized the pets wouldn't give them any useful information (as they could not talk, and if they could they wouldn't anyway).

"Is this even legal?" Wendy asked annoyedly. She was hungry, tired, and thirsty, which all contributed to her irritation. "I mean, aren't we technically their hostages?"

"This is stupid," Justin muttered, who was also experiencing strong irritation. "Why do I have to be waiting outside all day with a bunch of animals, even if they can do weird stuff?" Watt looked offended, and glared at Justin as he started to crackle with electricity. Fade extracted her claws and hissed loudly, flashing on and off between invisible and visible.

"Watt! Fade!" a tired voice called. "You mustn't be disgruntled with the misguided opinions of others."

"Misguided opinions?" Justin yelled angrily. "If you're the idiot who's trapping us here, I wouldn't be so upset about misguided opinions! Show yourself! Who said that?"

"That would be me," responded the voice. After a moment of frantic looking, they finally realized where the voice was coming from: above. A man stood on a small cloud floating in midair right above them, presumably the same cloud that Watt had created as a message. Watt and Fade stopped snarling and looked up at him like obedient soldiers at war.

The man was wearing a ragged robe, and he had bags under his eyes. He was riding on top of a solid cloud, no doubt the one that Fade had sent. But Teddy noticed something extremely unusual about him. He was carrying a staff topped with a shimmering magenta crystal. "My name," he said, "is…"

"Hermes Willowlands!" Teddy realized. The one and only Hermes Willowlands stared at Teddy suspiciously.

"Why, yes, Teddy," he said. "How did you know?"

"Your crystal," Teddy said. "It was on the news; it said that a bunch of bandits tried to rob that gem from a man named Hermes Willowlands… and… how do you know my name?"

"A simple Mind Reading Spell did the trick. Such an observant one, you are," Hermes said and smiled, but then it quickly faltered into a frown as he began talking to himself. "Oh, no, the whole world might know about it now. They mustn't know… but, I suppose a few extra people looking for those criminals won't hurt."

The three cousins stared at the strange man. "So… you're a real wizard?" Wendy asked.

"Sorcerer," Hermes corrected her. "We used to use the term wizard, but some people thought it wasn't as gender inclusive, so we changed it."

"I'm not an idiot," Justin spat. "Wizards aren't real, and that's the stupidest thing I've ever heard!"

"Sorcerer," Hermes said slightly more forcefully. "Please don't disregard us. And I do have magical powers."

Justin glared at him with malice. "Go on then, prove it."

Hermes Willowlands raised his staff high, and the Thunder Crystal began to glow. The three cousins stared dumbstruck as it gathered energy, and became brighter and brighter. Then, when it seemed that it couldn't possibly hold any more power, a ghostly magenta bolt flew out of the crystal, rose up into the sky, and created a semi-transparent flare. A few seconds went by, and then hundreds of non-transparent multi-colored fireworks flew out of the staff, soaring high into the sky and lighting it up with shades of the rainbow.

When it seemed the display couldn't get any more magical, a huge blast erupted from the Thunder Crystal, and a firework of gargantuan proportions exploded in the shape of a tall willow tree.

"I've always really had a thing with willow trees," Hermes Willowlands told them as they stood awestruck, mouths open wide. "That's when I chose my name: Hermes Willowlands."

"What do you mean?" Teddy asked. "You weren't born with that name?"

"Well, duh!" Justin replied rudely (although not without reason).

"Well, most of us aren't born sorcerers," Hermes explained. "Sorcerers who came from old sorcerer families usually have more... er, normal names than mine. I came from a very poor family. But then, when I was thirteen years old, I discovered the Thunder Crystal in the woods while I was taking a walk. That's when I found out about the whole world of magic and sorcery. I helped my family open a firework business (because that spell I just showed you was the first one I ever learned), and soon we were bursting with customers and money. Soon afterward, I enchanted Watt and Fade, who were just my pets at the time, so they could have magical capabilities and immortality. I gave Watt, this beagle right here, the power of lightning and storms. I gave Fade, this Bengal, the power of invisibility."

"You mean... there are more sorcerers?" Teddy gasped. It was extremely hard for him to grasp that he had been missing out on such a large and secretive portion of the world.

"Of course there are more of us!" Hermes scoffed. "A whole community, living in secret across the whole world! Sorcerers in America, sorcerers in Europe, everywhere!"

"Wow!" Teddy exclaimed.

"You really believe this?" Justin laughed. "This guy just knows a few magic tricks, and that crystal thing is probably just a firework starter!"

"Yeah, Justin's right Teddy," Wendy sighed. "I don't care if he knew your name, you have to stop believing in things that aren't real!"

"I don't mean to be rude, but I am indeed a real sorcerer," Hermes Willowlands sighed, disgruntled; what measures would he have to resort to in order to prove to the two elder children that he had magical capabilities?

He flipped his staff around, so the Thunder Crystal was pointing at Justin. Then, a bright flash and a ghostly magenta bolt fired out of it straight at Justin's heart. Suddenly, his green vest turned hot pink. Then, he pointed his staff at his purple t-shirt and it suddenly turned a very strange shade of maroon. "Hey!" Justin yelled. "Turn those back!"

Justin's face was ghostly white as if he had just witnessed an evil spirit. Teddy grinned so hard that it appeared that his face could never bend in any other direction again, and not just because of his cousin's embarrassment. He had always hoped that something amazing, incredible, and magical would happen to him, but he had no idea that it could happen so randomly.

Hermes Willowlands smiled and thumped his staff on the ground. The two ghostly magenta bolts flew out of Justin's t-shirt and vest and back into his staff, and the articles of clothing turned back to their original colors.

"Wow... so... you really can do magic?" Wendy asked, stunned.

"Of course!" Hermes grinned at her. "However, I am not a sorcerer of a magical bloodline, as I implied earlier. I need a magical artifact, like this crystal, for example, to be able to cast spells. Any of you three could just as easily cast a spell as I... of course, if you had the proper training. Here, Teddy, would you like to try?"

Teddy stared at him, dumbfounded, as the total stranger handed him his only weapon. "You seem trustworthy to me," Hermes answered his dumbfounded look. "Now go ahead. Try and cast a spell."

He raised the staff like he had seen Hermes do, and kind of wiggled it, expecting some sort of sonic boom. "It's all in the mind," Hermes whispered to him, and Teddy nodded in understanding. He pointed the staff at the willow tree and thought about what he wanted to happen as hard as he could...

A few seconds passed, and Wendy and Justin stared at him quizzically. Justin let out a hard laugh. "What a fool," he said. "He actually thought he could do magic! He actually thought..."

A large blast interrupted Justin's sentence and the staff that Teddy was holding let out a large fireball! It hit the willow tree and set the entire thing on fire! "Oh no!" Teddy gasped. "I was trying to make it grow!"

But on the contrary, Hermes seemed very impressed. "That was a very difficult spell you just used! The Fire Summoning Spell! You have got a lot of ability, you just have to learn how to control it. After all, the energy needed for magic comes from inside, and you are blooming with it!" The way he was smiling proved to Teddy that he was truly wowed.

"Thanks," he shrugged and handed the staff back to Hermes.

With a wave of his staff, the willow tree magically extinguished itself and returned to its normal state. "Now," he said very seriously. "I would have just let Watt and Fade evacuate you, but you have resisted. For that reason, I must take you up into the Purple Mountains myself."

"What?" Wendy interrupted. "The Purple Mountains? That range is miles away from here! You have to cross through Metronome Woodland and White Pine Forest to get all the way over there."

"Exactly," Hermes told them. "It's very secluded. We must get far away from this area."

"Why?" Teddy asked. "And we have to stay at home until Mom and Dad get back!"

"If you wait, then there won't be a home to go back to!" Hermes said hurriedly. "And I'm very sorry, but you will not see your parents—or hopefully anyone—for a long, long time. It is absolutely necessary for your survival! Now I do implore you, please follow me!" He began walking off towards their backyard, and into the forest that surrounded it: Metronome Woodland. The three cousins stood stock still. There was nothing that could persuade them into following a total stranger. Except for Teddy.

"Guys, he's a real sorcerer!" Teddy exclaimed. "We have to trust him!" He ran off after Hermes into the forest. Wendy and Justin hadn't moved an inch, so Fade started pushing Wendy forward, and Watt pushed Justin.

"Doesn't this technically count as kidnapping?" Wendy asked frantically, attempting to get out of the cat's grasp. "I could call the police on you for sure!"

"If you're wise, you won't, for that would be the most dangerous thing you could possibly do," Hermes said, not even bothering to look back at her. Wendy wasn't sure whether or not this was a threat, but it convinced her to be quiet.

"What about those criminals?" Justin asked with a hint of fear in his voice. "Didn't they run into Metronome Woodland when they escaped? Won't they find us? Also, didn't that news report say that you were kidnapped by them?"

"They are least likely to look in this area," Hermes responded absentmindedly. "They probably think that they ought to have seen me there by now. And the non-magic people are wrong, as usual; I simply disappeared into the Enlightened Mountains after the matter was settled. That is where I live, in case you didn't know." Justin realized that there was no way to change his mind and so closed his mouth despite his many complaints.

The six figures began their long trek into Metronome Woodland. Teddy was extremely curious about the ways of magic, and he had a lot of questions. "Exactly how many spells are there?" Teddy asked.

"Nobody knows!" Hermes said, somewhat excited to be sharing his magical knowledge with somebody else. "There's an infinite amount of possible spells you can cast. I think there are three thousand or so known spells, and around four hundred curses."

"Aren't spells and curses the same thing?" Teddy asked curiously.

"Not at all," Hermes informed him. "A spell is a quick and simple magical enchantment, and a curse is an enchantment cast onto a person, other living being, object, or even a place that lasts a very long time. Curses are also known to be a lot more foul. There's the curse that can turn a person into a werewolf, one that can make all dead beings in a graveyard come back to life, and so many others!"

"Okay!" Justin yelled. "I really don't care! But I noticed, you never told us why we're going on this crazy trip! Why must we go to the Purple Mountains!"

Hermes sighed. "I wanted to wait until you're out of danger, but I suppose you won't go with me until I tell you." Teddy, Wendy, and Justin perked up.

"It began long ago, just a few years before I acquired the Thunder Crystal," the sorcerer said animatedly. "It starts with the story of an organization of sorcerers from around the world: the Sorcerer Council. Actually, its official name is the Official Worldwide Sorcerer Council for the Removal of Illegal Magic, but then everyone started calling it the O.W.S.C.R.I.M. for short, but now in this day and age it is just known as the 'Sorcerer Council'.

"The Sorcerer Council is the main reason why humans incapable of magic still don't know that magic exists. We keep it secret, as it has become far too dangerous for normal people to use. However, at the same time, we need to keep magic alive by teaching others how to use it. When a sorcerer recruits a non-magical person (this would be because they detect magic in the person) they become their apprentice and travel with them until they become a graduate of magic. However, we cannot recruit too many normal people at once, for then there is a greater risk of the non-magic population discovering the existence of sorcery. Anyway, as I said before, the Sorcerer Council is mostly in charge of keeping all of this a secret, but this became very hard when a beast called the Oracle came to life.

"She was an awful creature, a monster. She set off to destroy the world, and the Sorcerer Council decided that she had to be stopped. However, the main reason why everyone was afraid of the Oracle at the time was because she was created by the Sorcerer Council.

"It was one of the biggest mistakes we ever made. It was before I had acquired the Thunder Crystal. In fact, it was even before I was born. The lord of the Sorcerer Council was Lord Jenna Everest at the time, and..."

"Lord?" Wendy interrupted.

"Yes, the Sorcerer Council elects a leader who will lead for the rest of their life," Hermes explained. "Then, after their death (or, possibly, if we feel the need to deselect them), we elect a new leader. The leader is called our lord. Don't ask why, it is a very old tradition.

"Anyway," he continued, "Lord Everest was not a bad lord, but... she made some mistakes. Dark sorcery was very common at the time, almost as common as it was in the Middle Ages. Lord Everest saw people dying, innocent ones becoming corrupted, and even those without access to magic being murdered.

"Yes, Lord Everest saw all of these things, but her idea of how to stop them was definitely not the best solution. She used the infamous book, *Magic of the Dark Moon.*"

"What's the Dark Moon?" Teddy asked.

"I apologize," Hermes said. "Most non-magic people call it the new moon. Whenever there is a night where no moon is present to shine down its light on the earth, very dark magic is produced. *Magic of the Dark Moon* is a book composed long ago by sorcerers from medieval times. It contains all of the known spells that are fueled by the Dark Moon.

"Lord Everest looked through the entire book, looking for something she could use to fight back against the horrible dark sorcerers, and then, she finally found a spell that could work.

"It was a spell that could create a ruthless, magical soldier that would obey their creator's every command. And so, on the next Dark Moon, she cast this spell and created the very first witch. She cast spells for more witches and realized that there were four main types: Fire Witches, Earth Witches, Air Witches, and Ice Witches. Each type fought with the powers of its element. The next Dark Moon, she made hundreds, and then on the Dark Moon after that, she made hundreds more. But then, on the seventh Dark Moon she created a very strange and different witch.

"This witch was much more powerful than the rest, standing at a height of twelve feet. Lord Everest named her the Oracle. However, she was not a mindless slave like the other witches. She was greedy and wanted the unstoppable army of elements for herself. She attacked the Sorcerer Council and attempted to kill Lord Everest, begging to find out how to control the witches. Lord Everest didn't know, so the Oracle cast her own spell on the next Dark Moon.

"The Oracle, being much more powerful than Lord Everest, cast a spell for a much stronger witch, who became known as the Elder Witch. He could control the other witches, and so he became the Oracle's second in command. The Oracle had no heart, and she was a ruthless killer. She only wanted the power of the universe. So, she set out to destroy the magical world.

"Most non-magic humans didn't know about the Oracle's reign, because she wanted to destroy the sorcerers first. But if

Michael Nightwhale hadn't stopped her, they would have, and none of you would be alive."

The three cousins stared at him. Justin's mouth hung open half in disbelief, half in fear. Wendy's eyes were the size of dinner plates. Teddy was grinning in triumph over his cousins' expression, but he too was nervous.

"So... are you saying... that thing could return?" Wendy gasped. Hermes nodded.

"Michael Nightwhale trapped the witches in the Thunder Crystal, and I guess that those bandits didn't break out just to rob a bank or something else. If they can get their hands on the Thunder Crystal, and bring it back to the place where Michael Nightwhale cast the Interdiction Curse on the Oracle (which happens to be the village where you reside, Teddy), they will be able to release the Oracle!"

"Why would they want to do such a thing?" Teddy asked bewilderedly.

"They think that the Oracle will reward them in some way," responded Hermes grimly. "However, we all know that she won't, because the Oracle is mindless and evil, as she was created to be. Those who think otherwise are very foolish."

Silence followed Hermes's statement. "Now, I must report to the Sorcerer Council on how our mission is going," he told them. "Clearly, since I had to come down here to escort you to the Purple Mountains myself, it isn't going very well. Lord Knotweigh will not be pleased..."

He continued to mutter to himself as he raised his staff and waved it around. All of a sudden, a large, blank, television-sized screen appeared a few feet away from them, floating in mid-air like some sort of ghostly mirror.

The Thunder Crystal suddenly lit up and shone a bright light onto the white screen like it was a movie projector of some sort. And, also like a movie projector, it turned the blank canvas into surprisingly realistic imagery. Except all they could see was just mist and fog, like the projector had clouded up.

But then, Hermes spoke loudly and clearly, "The Council Room, Nightwhale Castle."

As if it had heard him, the fog swirled into a giant whirlpool in the ocean. Then, the whirlpool turned into a large city in what looked like Japan.

"It's trying to find the specific place that we're looking for," Hermes said to Teddy, after seeing his confused expression. After the Japanese city, it formed into a blooming seaside village in Italy, then what Teddy recognized as the Berlin Wall.

"Ah, we're getting close," he told the cousins with a twinkle in his eye. "Nightwhale Castle, which is the place where the Sorcerer Council meets, is in the Black Forest in Germany."

Then, a dark, foggy, fairytale-like forest came into view. After that, a castle formed in its place. And as that swirled out of view, the meeting room came into view as many faces stared at them.

"We're here," Hermes smiled.

Five

A Message To Nightwhale Castle

In the Council Room, eleven people faced them. These people sat at a long, narrow table, which appeared to be made of beautifully polished red mahogany wood. On the sides of the table, there was a gold rim, with pictures carved into it that looked somewhat like Egyptian hieroglyphics, only featuring sorcerers in various time periods.

The room was about fifty feet tall, with fancy forest-green colored marble walls with flags from countries all around the world on them. On the back wall, there was a large stained glass window featuring the first lord of the Sorcerer Council, Isaac Nightwhale (although Teddy did not know this).

There were two other tall windows on the left and right of the stained glass window that stretched almost from floor to ceiling. Outside, Teddy could see the foggy Black Forest. The view stretched out for miles, but any civilization nearby was left unseen. The two windows let in long shafts of silvery light, as they were the only light source of the room besides a lavish emerald chandelier hanging above them all.

At the head of the table near the opposite side of the magical television, there was a throne-like chair made of pure blue diamond. In that chair sat a middle-aged and very stern-looking sorcerer.

He was bald, tall, slim, and had very thick gray eyebrows and a matching gray beard. He wore a plain black robe that could have been mistaken for a work suit and had clean rectangular glasses perched on his pointed nose. He would have had an aura of power even if he hadn't been sitting on the fancy throne made of diamonds, and he was someone Teddy decided never to argue with.

"Is that a pirate or a lumberjack?" Justin asked somewhat loudly and rudely. "Either way he's freaking me out."

"That's the lord of the Sorcerer Council, Gregor Knotweigh," whispered Hermes quickly before the odd boy could say another word. The sorcerer stared at Lord Knotweigh intently. Obviously, he was not allowed to speak until asked to.

"Oh," Justin said, slumping. "Well, a dictator was my next guess and that's close enough, I suppose."

Sitting next to Lord Knotweigh were two women, across from each other. One of them had dirty blonde hair pulled into a bun and a maroon robe that was ripped and frayed. She had a stiff expression and was staring at the mahogany table. The woman opposite of her looked like a slightly younger version of her. She had a fancy purple dreamlike robe and messy golden hair. Unlike the first woman, she was smiling nervously and looking around at her fellows. Teddy noticed that the two women looked so facially similar to Lord Knotweigh that they just had to be his younger sisters.

"Mercury and Gina Knotweigh," Hermes whispered to him, proving his theory. "They're Officers. It's the second-highest ranking of the Sorcerer Council. Those four sorcerers next to them are the Masters, a slightly lower rank. Then, there are the eight Patrollers, who are the lowest ranking. That's what I am."

As Teddy looked more carefully, there appeared to be fifteen seats, but only eleven people. Two of the Masters were missing, and Two of the Patrollers were missing. Then, he realized that one of those empty seats belonged to Hermes.

After an even closer inspection, he realized that all of the seats were made out of different materials based on rank. Mercury and Gina Knotweigh's seats were made out of gold, the Master's seats were made out of silver, and the Patroller's seats were made out of bronze.

"Hermes Willowlands," Lord Knotweigh spoke in a low, powerful voice. Teddy jumped; he had been looking around the room inattentively.

"I see your initial plan failed," he said, nodding his head toward the children.

"Yes, well, they resisted my pets' evacuation plan," Hermes said nervously.

"And they were the only ones in the area?" Lord Knotweigh asked.

"Yes, of course, my lord," Hermes said defiantly. Watt and Fade nodded vigorously from behind him. Lord Knotweigh leaned back in his seat with his hands folded in his lap, pondering the case.

He sighed. "Well, I see no real harm done, so you may continue with your mission—"

"I object, my lord," one of the Masters interrupted in a bossy voice. She was a young woman with black hair in a ponytail and a long red robe that fell to her feet. But her most surprising feature was a long gold staff with a red crystal at the top. The crystal appeared to be levitating a few inches off of the staff like it was a magnet gently repelling against another, the gold staff being the second magnet.

Lord Knotweigh looked surprised. "Do you have a problem?" he asked politely, although his voice had gotten angrier.

"I certainly do," she declared.

Hermes sighed exasperatedly. "That's Ruby Hailheart," he told the cousins. "That crystal right there is a Shapeshifting Crystal, giving her shapeshifting abilities. Never trust her, she's short-fused, hot-headed, and somewhat shifty." At first, Teddy thought this was a joke and laughed, but Hermes's face was dead serious, and Teddy began to feel a bit nervous.

Ruby Hailheart continued. "We have given that idiot too many second chances!" she yelled, pointing at Hermes rudely. "He's wronged us time after time, and we just keep forgiving him! Do you not remember the time that sorcerer with that Storm Crystal threatened our council, and that nitwit accidentally cast a Wind Spell? Like that helped our situation at all?"

There was a murmuring among the Sorcerer Council. Hermes turned bright red. "Now, now, be reasonable, Ruby," a Patroller responded. He was middle-aged and squat, with a kindly face and a long wooly beard. He wore a bottle green robe and carried a staff with a crystal in a similar shape to the Thunder Crystal, only lime green.

"Rubus Woolsberry," Hermes told Teddy.

"Yeah, that was a tough day for all of us," a woman with neat black bangs and a blue robe responded. "I don't remember you being much of a help… unless you count getting swept up in the whirlwinds as a sparrow."

A Chinese woman with a wooden staff topped with a yellow crystal chortled loudly as Ruby Hailheart muttered something that sounded like "unintentional" under her breath.

"Silence, please, all of you," Lord Knotweigh responded. "But Daffodil is right. We all suffered that day, and unless you have a further point to make, you may sit down."

Hermes gave a thumbs-up to Daffodil Coolwater, the woman in the blue robe, and she did the same to him. Clearly, they were good friends, especially since Hermes's empty seat was right next to hers.

Ruby Hailheart stuttered for a few moments and then sighed. However, some of the other members still had things to say. "I don't think Hermes Willowlands should be trusted with something this big," a woman with a strong French accent said. "I mean, this is the Oracle we're talking about. She was the biggest disaster that ever happened to our council."

At this, more murmuring broke out. Ruby Hailheart looked delighted at finding something else to persecute Hermes with. "Yes, that was another point I wanted to make," she said in her bossy voice.

Rubus Woolsberry looked worried. "Come now, if we think that Hermes can't accomplish this task, who really can?" Daffodil Coolwater spoke out.

"I bet I could do it," grumbled a tall, young Scottish man.

"We need someone with more experience," the Patroller with the French accent said. "Who would be worthy of the job?"

"I'll gladly take his place," the tall Scottish man spoke again. He wore a smock-like cloak with its sleeves rolled up, and he had a red bandana tied to his head. He also held an African helmeted turtle and was gently stroking its shell. "I've had experience! Put me in!"

"You might even be worse, Hex Turtlerod," Ruby Hailheart sneered. "Walking around, stroking that idiotic turtle of yours! You don't even have magical ability, you rely on that pesky little familiar!"

Teddy could see she was right, as the turtle began to spark, and started shooting miniature flames all over the place.

"Silence, Ruby!" Lord Knotweigh cried. "And Hex, put out your turtle! How can we make decisions with your immature shenanigans?!"

Ruby Hailheart started to growl somewhat animal-like and raised her staff in anger. At first, Teddy thought that she was going to curse Lord Knotweigh, but then he remembered she had a Shapeshifting Crystal. So instead, after she had raised her staff, it disappeared in a blinding flash of red light.

Teddy looked around wildly, but when the light cleared, both the staff and Ruby Hailheart had disappeared. Instead, on the table, there was a very angry honey badger, snarling and gnashing its teeth.

"Ruby, control yourself!" Lord Knotweigh yelled at her angrily. There was another flash of red light, and Ruby Hailheart appeared back in her seat with her staff in her hand, looking extraordinarily grumpy.

"Now, are there any other objections to Hermes continuing his mission?" Lord Knotweigh asked.

Silence followed this statement. Gina Knotweigh smiled, but Mercury Knotweigh continued to stare at the table with a stiff expression; neither of them had said a word yet.

But then, Mercury Knotweigh stood up. "I believe that the past can and will repeat itself," she said. Her voice was cold and cruel like she was talking to a revolting and vile creature. "Hermes has proved himself to be a kind, yet foolish person... he will blunder the mission just as he has blundered dozens of others."

"What are we supposed to do?" Gina Knotweigh asked, finally speaking. Her voice had to be the direct opposite of her sister's, as it was warm and kind, but also had a hint of nervousness. "Will we just hide and wait until the Oracle finishes off the world? Who in this room can fight the Oracle better or worse than Hermes Willowlands? I'm surprised he even took the job, as he's likely to die in the process... I say, if he wants it, the mission will be his!"

"Here, here!" Daffodil Coolwater yelled, and Rubus Woolsberry nodded vigorously. The Scottish man with the turtle, Hex Turtlerod, muttered something to himself annoyedly, but he seemed nervous enough by Gina Knotweigh's statement that he didn't object.

"He's amazing at magic!" Teddy blurted out. The whole council stared at him. "Sorry," he whispered to himself, but Hermes smiled at him.

So did Daffodil Coolwater. "Well, the boy has spoken," she said, grinning. "I think it's time to cast our votes, Lord Knotweigh."

Gregor Knotweigh looked surprised, but he straightened up. "All in favor of revoking Hermes Willowlands of his mission?"

Mercury Knotweigh slowly raised her hand, and the French woman followed. Ruby Hailheart raised hers so fast she almost hit Gina Knotweigh (who sat next to her) in the ear.

"And, all in favor of keeping Hermes Willowlands as the one to carry out the task?" Lord Knotweigh asked. The rest of the Sorcerer Council, including Daffodil Coolwater, Rubus Woolsberry, Gina Knotweigh, and even Hex Turtlerod raised their hands. Watt and Fade were jumping up and down maniacally. Even Teddy raised his hand, even though he assumed that it wouldn't be counted into the vote.

"All right, then," Lord Knotweigh declared defiantly. "Hermes Willowlands, you will keep your job, and you will continue into the Purple Mountains until you are all safe from danger. Then you will track down those bandits and make sure they can't steal the Thunder Crystal."

Mercury Knotweigh stared down at the table, her expression unchanged. Gina Knotweigh looked a great deal happier than she had been before. Ruby Hailheart looked livid.

Hermes nodded, unable to hide his grin. But then, his face fell slightly. "Lord Knotweigh," he asked, "if, by chance, the Oracle does come back... must I handle her army by herself?"

Ruby Hailheart nodded defiantly, and Lord Knotweigh looked at him quizzically. "Why, of course not," he said, and Hermes's worried expression disappeared. "All we're asking of you is to evacuate the area where the Oracle can return from, and rescue the non-magic people! If the Oracle does return, reinforcements will be sent."

Hermes smiled now. "Thank you, my lord."

"Good luck to you," Lord Knotweigh said. "Oh, and one more thing. Watch out for Orion. Though we banished him and his cult of followers years ago, he is said to still roam the forests of Alaska."

Hermes Willowlands nodded. He raised his staff once again and then tapped it hard on the ground. The Council Room faded out of view, and then came the random flashes of the world. There was a space station, then a town square, and finally a little pond before the television-like screen disappeared, and the Thunder Crystal stopped projecting images. Hermes Willow-lands sighed and continued to walk.

"That certainly could've gone better," he muttered.

"Why?" Wendy asked. "I mean, you kept your assignment!"

"There wasn't even supposed to be a trial like that," he said gloomily. "The whole point of that message was to prove to them that I had succeeded in collecting you three. But of course, Ruby Hailheart and the others had to make it into a fiasco."

"Hermes, who is Orion?" Teddy asked.

Hermes looked uncomfortable. "Titus Orion is a former Sorcerer Council Lord, and the only Lord to have been banned from sorcery. You see, Orion was a reckless man… he didn't care who lived or died as long as the council triumphed. Although he had many supporters among the sorcerers since he greatly increased the triumphs of the magical people, the council saw his carelessness and decided to elect a new Lord. Gregor Knotweigh was his second-in-command Officer at the time, so he became the new Lord. A lot of sorcerers were against that decision; obviously, many still viewed Orion as a king. But, Lord Knotweigh is a serious, tough man, who could handle him; many individuals on the council at the time were corrupted by Orion's rule, and even those who supported Lord Knotweigh attempted to overtake Orion with violence and cruelty. Only Gregor Knotweigh responded calmly and intelligently to Orion's insubordination to the Sorcerer Council. He banished him and brought back the magical community from nearing its end. The government was already unstable after Lord Everest's rule, and Orion, among others in the council, nearly collapsed it. Thus, no matter what my opinion may be of Gregor Knotweigh at the moment, I will always respect him for bringing back the Sorcerer Council from Orion's grasp. In fact, before Marco Victor Odious escaped from prison, we were in a bit of a golden age under his rule. Anyway, Orion is said to roam the most isolated forests with a cult of his followers. He carries multiple magical objects, so he would be a great threat if he decided to take over. However, I think that the takeover of Titus Orion is unlikely... for now."

They continued to walk on, as Hermes muttered to himself. As they continued, it began to get colder. Chilly winds blew at their faces and growled in their ears. Teddy shivered but continued walking, while Justin complained and muttered to himself. Hermes kept on going without showing the slightest notice of the change in temperature, as he was still grumbling about the meeting. However, as dark clouds crowded the sky, he finally spoke to them.

"It is getting late," he said. "We must stop here tonight and continue on tomorrow."

"What?" bellowed Justin rudely. "We're not going home now? What kind of madman are you?"

"Surely you didn't think we would only escape for one night! If you don't wish to be killed viciously by the Oracle right after being tortured for her entertainment's sake, I would advise you to come with me," Hermes said to him coolly; he was exhausted, and dealing with Justin seemed to drain him of energy even more. "Besides, with night approaching, I'm not sure you would be wise to wander out into the cold in an Alaskan forest."

Teddy smiled as Justin spluttered. "Hermes, where will we sleep?" Wendy asked.

"I will conjure us up tents," he replied defiantly. Wendy seemed to understand that there was no use arguing, and Justin was still tongue-tied.

Hermes raised his staff, and five ribbons shot out of the Thunder Crystal. They twisted and turned, and finally morphed themselves into five small, bottle green tents. Hermes crawled into the nearest one, and Wendy and Justin quickly jumped into tents far away from him. On the contrary, Teddy picked the tent closest to him, and he heard Watt and Fade clamber into another tent, curled up together to obtain heat.

As Teddy knew, the Alaskan winds come and go as they please, and at that moment they decided to come. They chilled their bones and made them shiver, but inside, Teddy was not nearly as cold as the others were.

As the wind whistled outside, Teddy smiled as he realized how dramatically his day had changed. Then, he curled up into a comfortable position and fell asleep. However, none of them noticed the three mysterious figures lurking just outside of their view.

Six

The Three Travelers

Marco Victor Odious stood alone in the middle of the forest clearing which he had made into a base. Walls of sticks and stones lay in a circle around the clearing, not completely obscuring it from view, but still making it difficult to climb over. He was quite still and sour-looking, completely lost in his thoughts. But then, a crackle from just behind the wall burst out, and he jumped. However, he quickly straightened up when he realized it was just his three faithful henchmen.

Dylan McCamel, Michelle Laurens, and Shannon Jones clambered over the wall that Marco Victor Odious had forced them to create. He looked at them with an annoyed expression on his face.

"Well," he barked, "do you have any news for me?"

"Yes," Michelle Laurens peeped exhaustedly; all three bandits had bags under their eyes, as they had spent the whole night hiking back to the clearing.

"Then, why don't you tell me what it is," he said aggressively.

"Hermes Willowlands is heading towards the Purple Mountains," Dylan McCamel said quickly.

"Ah," Marco Victor Odious sighed sneeringly, stroking his goatee. "This confirms my suspicions. You have done well... for now. Now, you must go and obtain the Thunder Crystal! However, do not do so until they are extremely far away from the village... otherwise, that idiotic sorcerer may get back in time to stop us from unleashing the Oracle."

The three bandits sighed; they had been hoping to rest. Grudgingly, they climbed back over the wall and set off again. "Now, I must leave. I must go and inform my... assistant," Marco Victor Odious said to the three of them.

They stopped in their tracks. "Master Odious?" Shannon Jones asked. "Could you please... could you please tell us who this 'assistant' is?"

He laughed cruelly. "Do you honestly think that I will tell you? No, you will find out when the time comes; otherwise, you would spoil the plan. But before that, none of you shall know... alive." Marco Victor Odious muttered that last word with a hungry look in his eyes.

The bandits took off towards Hermes Willowlands once again, and Marco Victor Odious, laughing maliciously, started a journey of his own.

Meanwhile, as the sun rose, Teddy, Justin, Wendy, Hermes, and the two pets awoke. Teddy climbed out of his green tent and yawned. Hermes Willowlands was already up and gathering sticks to start a fire since it was still quite chilly outside.

Teddy began gathering sticks too, and even Watt and Fade joined in. Fade picked up sticks in her mouth, purring contently, and Watt simply created a magical cloud that scooped up sticks and threw them into a pile. Hermes lit the fire with a small magenta fireball that erupted from his staff.

After the glimmering pink fire had been lit, Justin and Wendy (who had been hiding in their tents to avoid picking up sticks with Hermes and Teddy) came out, yawning widely and grumbling.

"Good morning," Hermes said politely to the two of them as he sat down next to the large fire to warm his hands. "We will be leaving shortly to continue our journey to the Purple Mountains."

Justin moaned loudly. Hermes pretended not to notice, but Teddy could see a glimmer of annoyance in his eyes. "What's for breakfast?" Wendy asked. She was obviously trying to cover up Justin's rudeness with a simple question, but Hermes found this just as insulting.

"Well, I don't know," he responded. "We'll have to catch something, I suppose."

Justin opened his mouth in anger, but made no noise. Even Teddy was confused. "Can't you just create food using magic?" he asked.

"No can do," Hermes responded sadly. "I'm sorry, but food spells haven't been invented. I can create things to help catch and cook whatever we find, but I can't just create food."

They found a blueberry bush and picked as many as they could. Their stomachs weren't full, but, despite Justin's complaints and Wendy's moans, they were ready to continue on.

"I wish I didn't have to go on this crazy trip," Justin muttered angrily. "All these insane sorcerers, and this 'Oracle'... how do we even know she exists?"

Teddy heard him, and responded in a huff, "If you don't believe Hermes, then shouldn't you believe those other sorcerers on the Sorcerers Council? They don't trust Hermes, and they believe that the Oracle exists."

Justin grumbled more but kept on walking. "Teddy," Wendy addressed him, "honestly, I believe that we should evacuate your village, but should we truly go towards the Purple Mountains? Why not go somewhere else? I mean, there's barely any food here and it's freezing. Why not a village somewhere else?"

"An excellent question, Wendy," Hermes said as he appeared next to her. "Watt could easily transport us on a cloud to a warm and safe village elsewhere. It is not because of you that we cannot do this; it is because of me. Sorcerers like myself are not allowed to show ourselves in the non-magic world. Do you think some people might find it suspicious that I was carrying around a staff with a crystal on it that emitted light, heat, and many other forces? The police would be called, and the staff would be out in the open for the bandits to steal. Why do you think I live in a cave at the top of one of the most dangerous mountains in the world? Sorcerers like me are safer away from prying eyes."

"I have another question," Wendy said. "Why can't Watt just transport us to the top of the Purple Mountains on a cloud?"

"Another good question," Hermes responded. "We could do that... but the force of it would weaken me. Since Watt's powers came from me and my crystal, they drain me of energy when they are overused. The journey to the Purple Mountains is a long one, and I would be incapable of magic for days, possibly even weeks... that would give the bandits time to obtain the Thunder Crystal. I'm especially weak because of the force it took for me to get here."

Wendy appeared slightly less annoyed with Hermes. Though her expression clearly showed that she wished for a much greater supply of food, Teddy could tell she understood why they were doing this.

"Hermes?" Teddy asked. "Please don't take this the wrong way, but I feel like you haven't told us what exactly we're up against."

"What do you mean?" Hermes responded curiously.

"I want to know, what are the witches' powers?" Teddy asked. "I mean, they can't be that awful..."

"One witch by itself is not a threat; however, the Oracle commands thousands of them," he responded. "As I said yesterday, the four types of witches are Fire Witches, Earth Witches, Air Witches, and Ice Witches. You can tell what type of witch they are by the amulet they carry and their eye color. Fire Witches carry red amulets and have equally red eyes. They can throw fireballs out of their... well, witches don't really have hands, but they throw the fire out of that general area..."

Justin rudely interrupted him. "They don't have hands? What do they even look like?"

Hermes grimaced; Teddy couldn't tell if he was grimacing because of the interruption or because he was envisioning a witch. "Well, they're horrible, awful creatures," he began. "Picture a large cloak floating in midair like there is a person inside of it with feet touching the ground that you just can't see… until you look inside the cloak and just see emptiness. The only real body part they have is their eyes, which appear to float in the middle of where their faces would be… underneath the hood."

Teddy shuddered as he pictured one. Hermes continued describing them. "The Fire, Earth, Air, and Ice Witches are all five feet tall. However, I'd say the Elder Witch is somewhere around eight feet tall, and the Oracle is an incredible twelve feet. She has a purple amulet and matching eyes, and she has hands, which are clawed and appear to be made of violet light…"

He stopped for a second to shudder. Even Justin and Wendy appeared to look very sickened by this description.

"Anyway, Fire Witches have red amulets and shoot fire," Hermes continued, though still slightly grimacing. "Earth Witches have green amulets and can summon thorns from beneath the ground and possess plants. Air Witches are the only types of witches who can float more than a few inches above the ground, and they can fly extremely fast. They have yellow amulets and shoot arrow-like clouds that fly at tremendous speeds. Ice Witches carry blazing blue amulets, and they can shoot ice rays and start snowstorms. With all of their powers combined and the fact that there are so many, they're a nearly unstoppable force to defeat."

They continued walking in silence. Minutes slowly ticked by as they walked through the frigid winds. After an hour or two, Teddy saw mountains in the far distance, although they were difficult to see because of the semi-transparent fog that loomed around them. It was also because of the fog that when Justin stopped abruptly, the group only realized it when Watt walked into him and zapped him accidentally.

"Hermes, I don't think we should be running away!" Justin told him. "Those things… those witches… they could destroy the world! People like us would be totally defenseless against them!"

"What are you saying?" Hermes asked suspiciously.

"I don't want to run away!" Justin cried out. "We ought to go and fight those bandits. And if they manage to get the Thunder Crystal, we have to fight the Oracle and the witches!"

For the first time in his life, Teddy agreed with Justin. "Hermes, I think he's right," Teddy pointed out. "If we can defeat the bandits, we'll all be out of danger! I have faith in you to help us."

Hermes Willowlands sighed. "You children don't understand. Marco Victor Odious is a criminal mastermind. If we just went up and decided to fight him and his bandits, he could defeat us brutally! He has trained tons of other criminals that could assist him too, even if it's his last resort, like Damien Komodo and Vincent and Ulysses Rogers…"

"But we have to try!" Wendy interrupted. "We can't just run away from our problems!"

"Even if we did have the skills and weapons to beat him, there's another problem," Hermes said with yet another sigh. "We have no idea where he is. He could be anywhere! I have my suspicions that he is somewhere in Metronome Woodland, but it's a very large forest, and he could be camouflaged! After all, he's a genius criminal!"

Teddy, Wendy, and Justin sighed. They still did not agree with Hermes that running away was the right idea, but they were running out of ways to argue; after all, he did have a point.

They continued through the mist, their legs aching. They had been walking for multiple hours, and were getting extremely tired. Teddy's back hurt and his ankles were sore, but they were no match for the battle going on inside his brain. Running away made him feel useless… he wished he could fight those bandits… he wished he could fight the Oracle… he wished he was home, and had never started the crazy adventure he was now forced to go on…

A large snap rang out from under their feet! Teddy looked down instinctively, and realized far too late that they were standing on a rope net! He yelled, and he heard his cousins shriek. The mechanical trap pulled up from underneath them, and before they knew it, they were stuck, hanging in midair in the wicked device!

Teddy swiped and clawed at the rope, but it was extraordinarily strong and his energy was wasted. "Hermes!" he yelled. He had no idea where the sorcerer was, as he was in the bottom of the net, his face pressed against the rope, which was cutting into his skin. "Hermes, can you get us out of here?"

"Unfortunately, no," he replied distractedly; he too had been working on trying to cut the rope. "When I heard the snap, I dropped my staff. Can you see it from your position?"

Teddy scanned the forest floor. He could hear Justin and Wendy rustle around, due to the fact that they were trying to search for the staff too. It was extremely foggy along the ground, and it was hard to see anything. However, Teddy peeled his eyes and saw the distinctive flash of magenta sparkling through the mist; it was the staff!

"I found it!" Teddy cried.

"Could you possibly reach it?" Hermes asked.

"I don't think so," he replied, straining his arm. "We have to be at least six feet off the ground."

"Can Watt or Fade get us out?" Wendy asked anxiously. Hermes was quiet as he thought about this. "Watt can't risk it; he could burn us to dust if he tried to strike the rope with a high-voltage lightning bolt. But Fade… she won't be able to get us out, but she may be able to hide us from sight… hunters may have set this trap, possibly even Marco Victor Odious. Either way, it's people that will want us dead. Fade, will you do the honors?"

Teddy could feel the Bengal cat nod her head from right above him. And then, a strange sensation came over him. A light layer of fog obscured his eyes, and at first he thought that the mist covering the ground had risen. But then, he looked at his hands… except he didn't have hands! The new magical fog surrounding him was just some sort of barrier that blocked him from view!

He looked around at the others, and although he didn't see them, he knew they were there because of the faint rustling noise they made as they too checked to see if they were invisible.

"And Fade… my staff, too?" Hermes asked politely. "If it truly was Marco Victor Odious and his malicious comrades who set this trap, then we don't want the Thunder Crystal to be in plain sight; it would be too easy to steal."

Teddy looked down and saw the glimmer of magenta fade away as it too became invisible. There was a few seconds of silence until Justin spoke up. "What do we do now?"

Hermes sighed. "All we can do is wait. And silently; we don't want to give our position away."

So, Teddy tried not to move or make any noise as the minutes ticked by. The wind blew at them, tossing the net around like a wrecking ball, which made him feel extremely airsick.

Teddy's arms and legs began to fall asleep from being in such an incredibly uncomfortable position for so long and he felt the rope of the trap scraping against his cheek. Then the hunger and thirst rolled in.

He had no idea what time it was but he knew hours had passed because a lack of water burned his throat. His stomach felt like it had been drained of all the blueberries he had eaten. It growled impatiently, which Teddy worried would give away their position.

However, the forest remained quite still. Another hour passed. It was now mid-afternoon, by the looks of the sun and the shadows, and Teddy was beginning to wonder if the person who had set the trap was ever going to come back to retrieve the six of them.

Then, there was a crackling in the distance, and Teddy froze. He told himself it was just a wild animal, which was not much better than the alternative. However, he heard faint voices coming closer... and closer... and closer! He could just barely make out what they were saying...

"We ought to stop soon," said a female voice that sounded like the speaker was around the same age as Hermes.

Another woman responded. "Are you joking? He could be hiding out just a few feet away, waiting to slit our throats as soon as we fall asleep!"

A much younger voice spoke out. "I'm starving. Didn't we set a trap somewhere around here? Also, Mother, I would appreciate it if we did not walk any further… it's getting late…"

The second voice erupted again. "April, it's not even dark yet! I'd say it's only about three o'clock!"

However, the first voice yawned. "I agree with April, Rowena. I'm tired, and we can continue looking for him in the morning."

By now, Teddy had realized that, thankfully, this was not Marco Victor Odious or any of the bandits. By the sounds of the conversation, it was a mother, a daughter who was around his age, and another woman.

Teddy's theory was confirmed as three people stepped into view. The first had medium-length curly blonde hair and black-rimmed circular glasses. She wore blue jeans and a plaid sweater.

The second woman, Rowena, was hard to see at first since she was wearing a dark camouflage shirt and matching pants. She was only visible by her vibrant shoulder-length red hair in a short ponytail. She was tough and formidable looking, and she was glaring at the curly-haired woman. She also carried a large, black backpack.

The third, April, was a girl who like Teddy had assumed, was around his age. Even if he hadn't listened to the conversation the three of them had been having, he would have been able to tell that she was the daughter of Rowena because of her red hair that fell to her waist. She wore a jade green sweatshirt and black sweatpants.

Then, she looked up right at the whole group, and Teddy froze, forgetting he was invisible. After all, even though they weren't the bandits, they could still be dangerous.

After looking up at them, April pointed defiantly. "I told you there was a trap here!"

"Unfortunately, it's empty," the curly-haired woman sighed. "I guess we'll have to find something else to eat."

But then, she tripped over and fell to her knees! "What the…" she gasped as she picked up her blue glasses. "I just tripped over something!"

"There's nothing there, Grace," Rowena said coldly. "Perhaps it was simply clumsiness."

"No, I definitely tripped over something," she argued. Grace bent over and started waving her arms around like she was blindfolded, attempting to find the thing that she tripped over when she accidentally stepped on the staff.

The force of the impact removed its invisibility. "Oh, my…" Grace gasped. "It's… it's…"

"What?" April asked curiously.

"It's the Thunder Crystal!" Rowena cried out. Hermes gasped. April heard him, and her eyes darted up and stared at the six of them! Teddy looked at his hand and realized that the Thunder Crystal was not the only thing that lost its invisibility; they had too!

"Mother! Aunt Grace! Look up!" she yelled. "The trap isn't empty!"

Rowena and Grace whirled around to look at them. Rowena instinctively reached into her backpack with incredible speed and pulled out a long dagger, which she pointed at the trap. "Are you, or have you ever been working for Marco Victor Odious?" she demanded.

"No!" Hermes shouted bewilderedly. "Who are you? And how do you know about Marco Victor Odious? Is it because of those wretched news reporters?"

Rowena lowered her dagger. "Oh, my..." she gasped. "Are you Hermes Willowlands?"

Hermes nodded, looking extremely confused; since he didn't have his staff, he could not perform a Mind Reading Spell to figure out how she knew this. "Did you know this from the news report?"

Rowena shook her head. "Then how do you know about me? How do you know about the Thunder Crystal? And again I ask, how do you know about Marco Victor Odious?" Hermes asked bewilderedly.

"You tell me your story first," Rowena said stubbornly, raising her dagger again. "What are you doing?"

"Mother, you're scaring them," April smiled. "And if we all lower our weapons and talk this out, I'll believe we'll find that our stories are, in some ways, the same."

Seven

An Odious Tale

Rowena sighed and put her dagger back in her bag. "May I have my staff?" Hermes asked politely. Grace handed it to him.

"I suppose I'll start at the beginning," Rowena began. "My name is Rowena Finnegan. This is my daughter April and my cousin Grace. We're searching for Marco Victor Odious."

The cousins and Hermes looked at them curiously. "Why are you searching for him?" Hermes asked. "He's a deadly criminal!"

"He's not only a deadly criminal," Grace responded. "He's also my brother. Which makes me Grace Odious." Silence followed this development in the story.

"But you're much younger than Marco Victor Odious!" Hermes said. "He has to be…"

"Thirteen years older," Grace told him. "And if you all stay silent for a few minutes, I'll tell you the story. Then we must make camp for the night."

She took a deep breath and began. "My brother was an amazing student. When I was old enough to fully understand my parents (as I was too small a child to comprehend full conversations until he was in high school), I learned that he was at the top of all of his classes. All of his teachers loved him; as I heard it, he was quiet, focused, and successful. He won awards for his academic excellence, and he was even in the local newspaper a few times. It's amazing how much people can change..."

Grace went pale and stopped talking for a few seconds. But, after the short pause, she continued. "However, there was always something strange about him; although I was too young to know it, he had a dark sense of humor, and a strange glimmer in his eye whenever he witnessed violence. Our parents weren't worried, as they were too focused on his good grades and his success.

"After he graduated from high school, he worked at a few local restaurants to help our family earn money; our parents weren't as young as they used to be, and raising me was too heavy a load on them. But, after a few years, despite our lack of money, they insisted that my brother should go to college. After all, as they had said, brains as big as his shouldn't be wasted.

"Though we did manage to raise enough money to get him into college, it was a very poor one. It was a small school in Texas, which proved to be a substandard one once he met Vincent and Ulysses Rogers there."

Hermes gasped. "Those two..." he muttered. Even Teddy found the names vaguely familiar. "I remember you mentioned them," he recalled. "I think I've heard of them elsewhere too,

I think it was on the news… aren't they wanted in, like, five countries?"

"Probably more," April sighed grimly.

Grace continued. "They were Marco Victor Odious's first-ever trainees, although they were fair criminals before that. The only reason they made it into college was because of robbing and looting. They were in their early forties at the time.

"When they met my brother, they knew he was one of their kind. The brothers told him of the schemes they had concocted, the crimes they had committed, and the havoc they had caused. Marco Victor Odious realized they had the right idea, and although he knew that they were complete idiots, they started meeting after classes every day. And even later after that, focused, successful Marco Victor Odious, the model student, started skipping class and failing to complete assignments.

"Like I said, he knew that Vincent and Ulysses were idiots, so he figured out ways to add skill and talent to their methods of crime. He studied the arts of war, battle, and thievery in order to increase his success in crime. He taught the brothers the knowledge he had gained from his research. That is when Marco Victor Odious began his long criminal record. He picked pockets, robbed houses in the dead of night, and burned buildings down. He never purposefully set out to kill anyone, but he would do away with anyone who, to put in his terms, 'got in the way'.

"I don't know what truly made him into the horrible person he is today. Perhaps it was his greed for money, or his want for fame. Obviously, he and the Rogers brothers dropped out of college, as they practically never even attended classes. But, not before someone caught him. A professor at the dreadful school caught the three of them plotting their next mission, and she quickly informed the authorities. The three criminals escaped together in the chaos of a police chase. They ran across three states, which wasn't just pure skill... After all, the Oracle was in power during that time, and even the non-magic people had their hands full with mysterious occurrences. Still, they were finally found, and..."

Grace turned even paler, took a deep breath, and continued slowly. "Here's the really scary part... It proves just how danger-ous my brother can be. Marco Victor Odious was cornered by twenty-three people. And no one knows what happened, but only eight of them escaped to get backup, and to tell the news station."

"Only eight? What happened to the other fifteen?" Teddy asked, dreading the answer.

"Rumor has it, the police jumped in their cars to avoid his blade, and he forced them off of a cliff with nothing but that same blade and a whip. The explosion of the cars was said to be seen from miles away," Rowena replied grimly. Justin and Wendy looked like they were going to be sick. All of the hope and happiness that he had ever experienced seemed to drain out of Teddy's heart. Even April, who had obviously heard the story before, trembled and looked as pale as a polar bear who hadn't seen the sun in years.

"My brother escaped after the horrible thing he'd done and began training other criminals, like Becca Foreman and Leonard Ruckson," Grace continued sadly. "And then, he met... him."

"Him?" Wendy asked.

"Damien Komodo," Grace replied. "Marco Victor Odious's most feared trainee. Today, he terrorizes the world with his gang, searching for a way to take over completely. He is said to be even more fearful and bloodthirsty than Marco Victor Odious himself."

"My brother taught him all he knew, and that's when he found out about the Oracle, informed by Damien Komodo's sorcerer assistant, Oscar Windwick. However, Marco Victor Odious was not interested in the Oracle at first. He, Oscar Windwick, and Damien Komodo and his followers found out about the Emerald of Eternal Life, a precious jewel that granted anyone who touched it an endless, painless life. Legend says they found said emerald in a dark cave in France, and Damien Komodo and his followers all became immortal. However, when it was Marco Victor Odious's turn to touch the emerald, Damien Komodo betrayed him. He grabbed the Emerald of Eternal Life and ran away.

"My brother, infuriated, then set out to bring back the Oracle, knowing that she was the only force capable of breaking the curse of immortality surrounding Damien Komodo, so he could finally get his revenge. He also believes that the Oracle will do as he commands when he frees her, as she will be grateful. But alas, if he does manage to free her, she will kill him if he so much as speaks to her."

Despair flooded into Teddy's heart. The seriousness of the situation seemed to echo through Justin and Wendy, too. A mass murderer was setting out to find an even more powerful entity with the capabilities to smite even those who had reached the point of being beyond mortal. After hearing this information, Teddy had much doubt that they would be able to stop them.

"We can't stop him," Justin concluded.

"We have to try," April said grimly. "But is there any way of stopping pure evil?"

"Well," Grace said, "I wouldn't say pure evil." Hermes, Teddy, Wendy, and Justin looked at her curiously. Even April perked up; she obviously hadn't heard this story. "After Marco Victor Odious destroyed those poor souls, he returned, very briefly, to my family's house. There, he made one last good act… he left us all of the money he had stolen."

Everyone gasped. "I got a good education and a true life because of him," she smiled sadly.

"But one good act cannot redeem him!" Rowena argued. "He's still a lethal murderer, even if he did save your family!"

"Well," Grace said, now frowning, "that goes without saying."

Everyone stared off into space, lost in their thoughts, until Hermes finally spoke. "So, the reason that you want to find Marco Victor Odious is to stop him, I presume?"

"Indeed," Grace said. "And if we can, then I wish for him to come back to our side, and be a good person, even if he is behind bars. I wish to bring back the love he used to have."

"I sense a problem in your ploy," Hermes sighed. "Is the creature that Marco Victor Odious has turned himself into even capable of love anymore?"

"We have to try," Grace begged.

Hermes contemplated this. "First things first," he decided. "We must get as far away from him as possible. And if there is a chance to bring him back… if it is possible… I'm all for it."

Grace thought this over. "Okay," she decided, smiling. Then, she thought for a few seconds. "I think I can piece together your story now," she said slowly. "The Oracle can only return through the Thunder Crystal... So that's why Marco Victor Odious is after you! That's why you were forced to flee!"

"Too true," Hermes sighed. "But I have to ask you to abandon your quest. Marco Victor Odious is a dangerous criminal, as I said before, he will show you no mercy. He may not even know what you look like anymore!"

"On the contrary, I have to ask you to abandon your quest!" Rowena shot back. "Because this man is so dangerous that he must be put behind bars! We won't stop until he is no longer a threat to the world!"

"What if we just follow them, mother?" April asked. "I mean, Marco Victor Odious is going to be following them anyway, so there's a large chance that we'll run into him! That way, we both get what we want! We get to find my second uncle, and you guys get to go... well, wherever you're going."

"The Purple Mountains," Teddy informed her. "And... that's a pretty good idea!"

Hermes agreed somewhat suspiciously. "I suppose that would work. Do we have an accord?" He extended his hand. Grace shook it, and Rowena followed a bit too aggressively.

"Wonderful," he said, clapping his hands together. "Now, as you said, we must make camp for tonight. We will set off together for the Purple Mountains, come tomorrow."

He raised his staff and created eight tents, this time a brilliant shade of electric blue.

"Sweet!" April said in awe. Teddy couldn't tell if she was so bewildered because it was her first time seeing magic, or she was just glad that she didn't have to sleep on the ground.

They all stretched, yawned, and crawled into their tents. However, that night Teddy did not fall asleep immediately. He was lost in thought about Marco Victor Odious. He wondered what could turn a smart and sophisticated young man into an absolute menace and a killer. He couldn't even bear to think about how he had managed to force those poor people off a cliff and into an explosion; whenever he did think about it, worry clouded over him and he started to think about how much longer he had in his life. He squirmed worrisomely in his tent for hours, until the sound of the wind and the crackling of canvas finally forced him to sleep…

The next morning, Teddy awoke extremely tired. Based on the bags under the others' eyes, he wasn't the only one suffering from lack of sleep.

After Rowena successfully hit a rabbit by throwing her dagger at an impressive speed, the others reluctantly cooked the poor creature over a fire; Teddy wouldn't have even thought about eating the pitiable rabbit if he wasn't so starving.

However, without a doubt, the small portion of rabbit he had gotten still strengthened him to continue the long walk to the mountains.

They silently trudged on through Metronome Woodland as it began to lightly snow. Their shoes crackled through the branches that almost completely obscured the ground as the light flurry of crystal flakes stuck to the trees and the ground.

Then, Hermes and the other adults stopped abruptly. April, Teddy, and his cousins (who had remained quite silent since the previous night) followed their lead.

"There they are," Hermes said with wonder in his voice. Teddy followed his gaze, and through the trees, he saw massive, snow-capped, rocky figures in the distance.

They were approaching the Purple Mountains.

Eight

The Journey Proceeds

A week had passed since Teddy and his cousins had begun their journey with Hermes. However, they were going much slower than Teddy had anticipated; they had only just made it to the Purple Mountains the previous day.

Part of the problem was caused by Rowena, Grace, and April. Whenever they stopped to sleep, the next morning they purposefully took until noon to get ready to walk again. Teddy assumed that this was because they wanted to make it easy for Marco Victor Odious to find them; they acted like Hermes was a magnet that would attract him, and they wanted to catch him as soon as possible. Hermes supported this hypothesis after Teddy had told him about it, but simply stated that there was nothing they could do about it, and that they couldn't abandon Rowena and Grace because they were extremely good at hunting (especially Rowena). April wasn't purposefully trying to sabotage the adventure (as she had developed a friendship with Teddy and Hermes) but she wasn't exactly a morning person, either.

Another part of the problem was caused by Wendy and Justin. The lack of food had made them all angry and irritated at times, but it seemed to be affecting the two of them the most. Both of them were used to being full and having to walk less than a mile a day. Wendy tried to be reasonable, but Justin, who was normally an irrational person, turned into an absolute menace. Hermes had to shake him aggressively each morning just to wake up when Rowena, Grace, and April were finally ready to leave. Teddy found this very strange, for though he had only known the sorcerer for a week, he seemed to be a calm and collected person who had never raised his voice before meeting Justin.

On the first few days, Teddy had liked the trip. However, now worry and anger clouded his thoughts. He was angry because Hermes had not used his magic to help them much; sure, he used it to help with hunting, and he cast spells occasionally to check to see if Marco Victor Odious was anywhere nearby, but other than that he did not use magic at all. Teddy knew that his intentions were good (Hermes just wanted to save his energy in case a real battle occurred) but it still aggravated him every day he had to walk, gather firewood, and find food without the use of magic.

Teddy was also bad-tempered at times from the lack of food, as they all were. Although he had grown accustomed to the small portions, they still made him wish that he had never agreed to go with Hermes.

His cousins exasperated him too, of course, almost as much as they exasperated Hermes. Their constant complaining, yelling, and irrational behavior made him want to abandon the quest completely. However, the thing that Teddy hated most was not the lack of magic, the lack of food, or his despicable cousins. It was the fact that he agreed with his cousins; he regretted going on the adventure and ever meeting Hermes Willowlands. He despised himself for despising the thing that he had always wished would occur in his life: magic. He hated that he wished it gone, that things would be back to normal, that he would be safely back at his house.

These feelings didn't even begin to mention the overwhelming fear that came over him day after day. He never believed that he would be running from a dangerous criminal, let alone a dangerous criminal searching for a way to unleash an unstoppable force of pure evil. Now that they were in the Purple Mountains, his worries doubled. Sleeping at night became nearly impossible due to the thunderous winds. His fear also kept him up; every time he heard a crackling in the forest from inside his tent, he didn't know what would be worse: Marco Victor Odious, a shadowy man with barely any conscience, or a mysterious and hungry creature of the night.

The third morning of the second week, Teddy woke up in cold sweats; the previous night he had dreamt that he was being chased through the woods by a massive cloud of darkness that obviously represented the Oracle. He zipped open his tent, and, as usual, he was the second one up. Hermes was stirring the magical fire, which was casting magenta shadows across the dark forest due to the fact that the sun was yet to rise.

"Good morning, Teddy," Hermes greeted him politely. Teddy walked over and warmed his icy hands. He looked up at the sorcerer's stoic and peaceful face. A question had lingered in his mind for the past few days, but he was worried to ask it. Hermes had been kind and collected around him so far, and Teddy did not want to test his patience. However, the question seemed to claw at his mind and his mouth, wanting to be asked.

"Hermes," he began slowly, trying as hard as he could not to be offensive. "Why can't the Sorcerer Council help us? I mean, if they just went and defeated Marco Victor Odious, we wouldn't have to go through with this."

A sour expression appeared on Hermes's face. "You saw what they're like," he said bitterly. "If you didn't notice from the meeting, I am respected by very few amongst the sorcerer community. The only people that rank lower than me on the Sorcerer Council are that reptile-loving Hex Turtlerod and the incredibly odd Tomasso Aristaios, and they both joined much more recently than me. I probably wouldn't even be on the Sorcerer Council if there were many sorcerers left…"

"What do you mean?" Teddy interrupted.

"We are sadly few in number," Hermes sighed. "There are not many of us left, due to a lack of magical artifacts. As you know, most sorcerers can be sorcerers only if they possess magical artifacts. The only people that can make magical artifacts are those who come from old sorcerer families, like the Nightwhales and the Knotweighs. Sure, there are still a few skilled magical engineers left like Edward Hydra (who happens to be a Master on the Sorcerer Council), Moira Solarnight, and even

Titus Orion, but that's not nearly enough to provide hope for the whole world of magic.

"Anyway, back to your original question, that's not the only reason we cannot call on the Sorcerer Council to help," Hermes continued. "In addition to that, they have their hands full momentarily. If you can believe it, Marco Victor Odious isn't their biggest problem at the moment."

"What?" Teddy asked bewilderedly. "The man is an insane killer who wants to unleash the Oracle upon the world!"

"I apologize," the sorcerer responded. "I should have been more specific. If Marco Victor Odious does manage to get his hands on the Thunder Crystal, defeating the Oracle will be their top priority. However, the Sorcerer Council believes that at the moment, Marco Victor Odious poses no huge threat. They are sadly mistaken, but you can see their point; there are much greater threats to the world of the sorcerers. Damien Komodo, of course, is still at large, and gaining in followers and power. And, of course Titus Orion is said to still be plotting his vengeance."

Teddy nodded. His answer had been reasonable, but he was not reassured. The truth sank into him; he realized that no help was going to come to them, and that he would have to get used to a life of running, hiding, and surviving in the wretched wilderness. Overwhelmed, he decided to go for a walk.

"Hermes?" he asked politely. "Should I go collect some firewood?"

"Yes, that would be nice, thank you," he said, smiling.

"I'll come too," a voice from one of the tents interjected, and April emerged.

Teddy sighed. He was hoping to clear his thoughts, but he supposed that having April with him wouldn't be so bad.

Together they walked into the darkness of the Purple Mountains. As the morning sun began to rise, it cast a pink and orange glow across the icy world.

"The Purple Mountains are quite a sight," Teddy said, attempting to break the silence. April nodded and looked at the scenery. Snow hung upon the trees like chandeliers, and ice covered the boulders that lay upon the earth here and there.

"How have you found the journey so far?" April asked him with a hint of sarcasm as they scanned the area for driftwood.

"It's been fine," Teddy said hesitantly.

She gave him a curious look. "You haven't been worried at all?"

Teddy hesitated, and then confessed. "I have been. Every night I just can't stop thinking about that horrid man and the malicious Oracle."

"Me too," she sighed. "I mean, me and my mother have been through a lot together, but it isn't something that you just get used to."

This statement sparked a question in Teddy's mind. "You and Rowena have traveled together, you say?" he asked. "What about your father?"

He regretted it as soon as he said it. "I'm sorry," he quickly said, suspecting the worst.

"It's okay," April sighed. "I expected you to ask. My father was an action-before-words man. Even more than my mother. He was brave, adventurous, and extremely opinionated. After he heard about the shame and devastation that Marco Victor

Odious had caused upon my mother and my family, he made it his goal to find and put him in prison. And so, he bid farewell to us all and set off on a three-week-long journey. That was the last time I saw him.

"Somehow, he managed to find him. From what I heard, he cornered him and yelled at the top of his lungs about what a despicable life-ruining man he was. Marco Victor Odious didn't even respond. He just smiled. We have no idea what happened next, but what we can imagine is... likely to be true."

Teddy stared at her. He was amazed that she managed to keep a straight face, although he could see the sadness inside her eyes. "I'm very sorry," he managed to say. "I wish I could say more, considering the circumstances, but it's hard to put in words..."

"I know what you mean," she responded. "Actually, I like this sadness... It gives me fuel. It gives me the power to accomplish my dream... to find Marco Victor Odious and ask him why he did that to my father... why he killed anyone... why he turned from such a smart young boy into a cruel man... and how?"

The sadness seemed to drain out of her as she said it.

"That's very wise of you," Teddy said thoughtfully. "But you're acting like you'll have to do it alone. I will assist you in any way possible... Marco Victor Odious has never personally wronged me, but I want my friend to be at ease in mind."

April smiled. "I'm extremely grateful," she said, pinching her nose to mimic his voice. "I wish I could say more, considering the circumstances, but it's hard to put in words."

Teddy laughed. "Come on, we should get some firewood now. The group will be wondering where we are."

After they had collected reasonable armfuls of driftwood, they made their way back to the camp. Teddy was absolutely amazed by April's bravery. Personally, if his father was murdered by a dangerous killer, he would want to get as far away from him or her as possible. And, if ever questioned about it, he would not have been able to form the words.

"Wendy is kind of freaking out," Justin told him tiredly. "I would've been able to get some more sleep if she wasn't screaming about how you could've been eaten by a moose or something… gee, thanks."

"There you are!" Wendy exclaimed with a frown on her face as she realized who Justin was talking to. From the looks of it she had just woken up. "I've been worried about you, Teddy! I don't care if Hermes let you go out without me watching you! Remember, both your parents and my parents agreed that I would have to watch over you…"

"I think the circumstances changed," Teddy shot back. "I can't see how you'll protect me from a practically immortal witch."

Wendy glared at him and stormed away. Teddy rolled his eyes, and April sympathized.

"I can see why they get on your nerves so much," she frowned. "She acted worse than my mother. And your cousin Justin, he's as stupid as he is annoying and lazy."

"At least someone understands," Teddy sighed. "But I can't be complaining, you've been through much worse."

"That's why I think you should give them a second chance," she continued gently. "While my father was alive, I thought he was annoying at times, or overprotective at times… I often rolled my eyes or became angry and irritated. But when he died… it was far worse. I regretted every time I scoffed at him. And I'm not saying that's how you will feel if one of your cousins dies; after all, my father had many good moments, but so far I've never seen your cousins be anything but nuisances. Still, there may be a time in your life where you will see reason to forgive them."

Teddy thought about this deeply. Then he laughed.

"What is it?" April asked, slightly offended.

"Nothing," he said, chuckling. "I'm just surprised that someone our age has so much wisdom."

April chuckled. "I've had my moments."

They put down the firewood just as the sun rose, casting shades of bright yellow and gold across the snow and the horizon.

Rowena and Grace awoke minutes later. They took one last look around their temporary campsite before they decided to set off. Hermes destroyed the tents. As always, Rowena and Grace insisted on keeping the magical fire burning with plenty of wood. They told everyone it was to find their way back home once Marco Victor Odious was behind bars and everyone was safe, but Teddy and Hermes knew that the real reason behind this was to give a trail for the criminal to follow.

Hermes did argue with them about this; leading Marco Victor Odious to them was a grave mistake, especially since Hermes owned the Thunder Crystal. However, they denied that the trail had anything to do with the criminal, and Rowena, being extremely stubborn and argumentative, was keen to go even further and tell Hermes that he was (in her words) a skittish toucan with no bravery whatsoever.

However, as they climbed higher and higher up the Purple Mountains, Hermes stopped arguing as much. He knew that these mountains were not nearly as dangerous as the Enlightened Mountains where he lived, but a fall or even a misstep could now severely injure one of them at this part of the journey. Luckily, he finally decided to boost their survival chances using magic through Watt and Fade.

The adorable electrical beagle created fluffy clouds that acted as elevators to lift them to ledges up to twenty feet above them that would have been impossible to reach otherwise. Fade, being a Bengal cat and excellent at jumping, occasionally jumped up some of the less steep ledges and helped others up by using her claws to grip onto them.

Now, when Hermes created the tents at night, they were so exhausted from the climbs that they collapsed as soon as they lay down to fall asleep. Teddy was not restless at night worrying, but this was arguably worse. His stomach growled from hunger, his feet pained from walking, and his arms, hands, and fingers ached from climbing cliffs all day.

Everyone was now constantly hungry, tired, and miserable. Not only did Justin slack in the mornings, but everyone (except Hermes who was an early riser, and Rowena who was as tough as iron) slept in and groaned at the thought of spending another day hiking and climbing.

Although Teddy had unusually strong upper-body strength and excellent climbing skills for his age, this was simply too much to handle, especially with the small portions of food. Another week passed, and school was starting again many miles away in the villages of Alaska. He would have been glad at the thought of missing school if this wasn't the other option.

After another day of climbing, his hands bled and his feet felt like they would fall off. April had deep bags under her eyes and she lay on the rocky ground, pained from lack of sleep. However, the trip seemed to be affecting Justin and Wendy the most (obviously). They had been forced to come, after all, and they practically looked like living skeletons.

Hermes sighed. "We must find a cave to sleep in," he said sorrowfully and looked around at his fellows. "I wish I didn't have to force you to do this. Especially you, my children."

Teddy acknowledged this comment with a nod, but everyone else was too weak to pay attention.

They walked around for a short while, trudging along, and finally found a cave. "Tomorrow we will not climb nor walk," he said, hoping to boost their spirits. "We must gain our energy back."

He created the tents, and Teddy dropped like a stone.

The next day, he woke up unusually rested. He opened his tent and it was midday. Hermes was awake as always, along with Rowena. It seemed that they had teamed up using his magic and her survival skills to kill some kind of deer, and they were now cooking it over the fire.

Teddy didn't even think about how it had given its life to feed him as he ate speedily; he was too hungry to think.

Others woke up and ate, but they soon went back to bed. However, Teddy stayed up a little bit longer, as something had caught his attention. A loud bird call came from just outside, and he went to investigate. He stepped outside and looked around.

There, he spotted a bald eagle nest perched on a tall tree that grew outside of the cave! There was only one there, but it was an utterly majestic creature. It flew off into the distance, and Teddy looked after it, and the scenery he saw was beautiful.

Mountains scraped the sky, snow glistened, and pine trees far below swayed back and forth in the wind. He finally realized why people would want to become mountain climbers, or why they would want to climb all this way at all.

He laughed at himself by how much more calm and appreciative he was when he wasn't under the torture of hunger and tiredness. But as he looked out, he noticed something strange.

Smoke burst up from certain places on mountains slightly below them, as if fires had been created. He first assumed that these were Hermes's magical fires, but he quickly remembered that one, they wouldn't last that long and two, the places that they were still burning weren't places that they had journeyed to so far.

He gazed around eerily, as if someone was watching him. He didn't know how he knew, but somehow he sensed that something was approaching him.

All of a sudden, an arrow flung out of nowhere and struck the ground next to him! He could hear voices and the sound of a large group of people approaching. He ran back into the cave at top speed, his heart pounding hard.

"Hermes!" he yelled. "I think he's found us!"

Hermes leaped into the air and peeked outside. He grabbed his staff. "Rowena, wake everyone up! Someone's coming!"

Thinking of Marco Victor Odious, Rowena excitedly woke up the others; this was the moment she'd been waiting for.

Justin, Wendy, April, and Grace all appeared with confused expressions on their faces. "What's going on?" Grace asked worriedly. Rowena shushed her loudly and put an arm around her daughter.

Hermes led them to the back of the cave, and Fade cast a shield of invisibility over all of them together. Then, a figure walked into the cave.

He was tall, with long white hair.

"No..." Hermes whispered. "It can't be..."

"What?" Teddy whispered back with fear. "Who is that?"

Hermes hesitated before telling him. "Orion."

Nine

Titus Orion

As the former Lord Orion stepped into the light of the fire, Teddy and the others marveled at his eccentric appearance.

He had long, crisp, blazing white hair that fell to his shoulders; the strange thing was, he didn't look nearly old enough to have white hair. He had a long, pointed nose and wore a brown robe. On this robe, he wore a leather belt that held a spyglass, a sword, and many different flasks filled with green, blue, purple, yellow, and red liquids.

However, his most eye-catching feature was, in fact, his eyes. They were both pure white and glowing, which cast small lights on the wall behind them.

Many more people stepped into the cave too. Teddy suspected that they were his followers. However, they didn't look particularly menacing; they looked just like normal people, although they all wore sorcerer robes and held either wands or staffs. There was a wide range of ages amongst them, the youngest being in their early twenties and the oldest being in their sixties.

"What is it, Lord Orion?" a young woman asked anxiously.

"Why are they calling him Lord?" Teddy whispered as silently as possible. "I thought he was banished?"

Hermes held an invisible hand to the boy's mouth to indicate to him to be silent.

However, Titus Orion did not seem to hear Teddy.

"I fear that we are not alone in this cave," Orion said in a raspy but official voice, like he was a leader making an important speech. "It is unlikely that a group would leave a fire going if they were leaving to go hunting. In fact, it is unlikely that anyone would be up on these mountains at all... unless..."

He looked over in the direction of Fade. His eyes seemed to cut through the invisibility, and Teddy wondered if he had x-ray vision. Then, he picked up a flask of blue liquid, hesitated for a moment, and threw it at Fade!

The invisibility shield around them dematerialized (Teddy could tell because he could now see the others) and Fade appeared to be slowly falling into a deep sleep. The blue liquid surrounded her and her fur and skin seemed to absorb it.

There were gasps from the people behind Orion. They had expressions of surprise and gratitude on their faces as if Orion had just found a cure for cancer.

"Wow!" an elderly man exclaimed.

"You're a genius, Lord Orion!" a woman cried out.

"Well done!" a young man yelled.

Orion smirked at this appreciation. "A simple sleeping potion did the trick… and now your poor little kitty is resting, Hermes Willowlands."

"I thought I would never see you again," Hermes glared. "The council banned you from going anywhere near any of the other council members, as you have a reputation for hypnotizing them, blowing them up, or putting them to sleep!"

The Thunder Crystal glowed, and Fade slowly stirred back to life. Watt ran over to his friend and helped her back onto her feet.

"You never really liked me," Orion snarled menacingly. "I bet you are beginning to regret that, now that your life lies in my hands."

Teddy expected to see one of the people behind him shout that he was unreasonable, and that he ought to be put behind bars if he was going to kill Hermes. On the contrary, many people hooted and hollered their approval. A few of them just nodded and stared into the distance with blank eyes. Although a few looked a bit skeptical, the peer pressure forced them to follow suit.

Hermes Willowlands didn't move an inch, and simply raised his staff in the air.

"I don't want to fight you," Hermes said forcefully. "We both know that you will win if we do fight, as you clearly have strength in numbers. But I think you will change your point of view when we tell you why we're here."

"I don't care why you're here!" Orion yelled. "You never realized that the greater good was worth fighting for! You and your foolish little friends are the reason I was banished. It cost me everything! And now, I have the chance to get revenge."

Scowling, he drew his sword. Now that Teddy could see it up close, he realized that the blade was coated in a strange purplish tint.

Orion smiled menacingly. "This sword is a magical invention of mine, as you know," he said to Hermes. "If it so much as scrapes your flesh, death by poison will come within the minute."

The kids gasped, and Justin even let out a shriek. Wendy quickly covered her cousins' mouths so that the attention of the madman would not turn to them.

"Do you know why we're here?" Hermes asked annoyedly, his patience running out. Everyone was shocked by his tone; he spoke as if he was discussing a matter with a stubborn coworker. Then, they remembered that Hermes and Orion were on the Sorcerer Council together, and Hermes had probably grown accustomed to speaking to him like that.

"You have until the count of three to explain yourself!" Orion yelled, his face as red as a ripe tomato. He raised his sword high in the air like a snake ready to strike. "One..."

"We are on this mountain to ensure that Marco Victor Odious does not obtain the Thunder Crystal," Hermes said quickly.

Orion stopped where he was, and his expression quickly changed from furious to interested.

"Are you certain?" Orion asked with a glint of mischief in his eye.

"Positive," Rowena interjected. "That's how we joined him."

Orion looked suspicious, and pulled out his spyglass. "This spyglass will show me anything in the world that I want to see," he bragged. "Another magical invention of mine. Now, let me see the truth."

He pointed the spyglass towards the opening of the cave and twisted a dial on the top. After a few moments, he gasped.

"He is here!" Orion exclaimed. "Not too far away, indeed…"

This last statement greatly raised Rowena's, Grace's, and April's excitement, and they peered outside of the cave like their relative was going to jump out at them at any moment. Justin and Wendy also looked around frantically, but in worry and fear instead. Teddy and Hermes, however, stayed invested in the conversation.

Orion began pacing, and his followers watched him eagerly, waiting for the brilliant idea that was to come. He muttered to himself as he paced, thinking hard. A lightbulb seemed to go off in his head; Teddy could tell because his expression changed to a large grin, and his eyes burned even brighter.

"We shall help you cross the Purple Mountains," he declared. His worshippers cheered and yelled at this.

"He's so kind and considerate!" one exclaimed.

"He was trying to kill Hermes a second ago!" Rowena yelled.

However, Orion took no notice of this and led them out of the cave. Hermes doused the fire, destroyed the tents, and followed along with everyone else.

Now that they were outside, Teddy could see that Orion only had about twenty followers, most of them around Orion's age (mid-forties). Most of them stared at the nine travelers in bewilderment that Orion did not destroy them (especially since

Hermes was present). However, Teddy noticed Orion tucked away behind a tree whispering to one other sorcerer, this one with long and gnarled red hair and an unshaven face. The young boy leaned his head in to listen.

"Marco Victor Odious will be overjoyed if you tell him that I captured Hermes Willowlands!" Orion whispered in excitement. "I want you to find him and bring him to me, so we can get rid of these fools once and for all!"

"Isn't that dangerous?" the man asked skeptically in a gruff voice. "Isn't he supposed to be a killer? And aren't you supposed to be one of his main enemies? I'm not afraid of a little bit of danger, but idiotic planning is another thing…"

Teddy stared at the man, thinking that Orion would surely threaten to abandon or even kill him for calling his planning idiotic, but Orion just shook his head which made Teddy assume that the man was somewhat high-ranking in the cult.

"Odious will come to me if you say that we have captured Willowlands," their leader responded confidently. "This is our chance to get rid of one of my main threats to my position as Lord of the Sorcerer Council. I cannot face Hermes by myself; his power has grown. We must do this. Do not fail."

Teddy gasped and quickly darted away from them. As the Orion-centered cult began to lead them across the mountain, Teddy tried to head for Hermes to warn him, but he didn't want any of Orion's comrades to overhear his suspicions, and there were too many of them.

Orion later returned to the group without the important red-haired sorcerer and took his place in front so he could lead the pack. He walked with an overconfident and obnoxiously important-looking strut, and his acolytes copied his every movement as if they were connected to a hive mind. Strangely, they began leading them down the mountain.

"Where are we going, Orion?" Hermes said, raising his eyebrows. "Is this another trick of yours?"

Teddy wanted to burst out and say that it was a trap, but he thought that the sword of Orion would end up through his heart if he so much as spoke a word against him.

"Certainly not," Orion said, although cautiously; if his plan failed and Hermes left him, Marco Victor Odious would do away with him for wasting his time. After all, he wasn't exactly a fan of his to start with.

"We are leading you to a secret passage through the mountains," he explained. "I created it all by myself when I decided to make a home out of these peaks."

Though many of his followers had helped create the passage along with Orion, they simply expressed their gratitude to their master. Teddy found it odd that no one had spoken up yet. Orion's followers were either as enthusiastic as optimists or they had a strange glassy-eyed stare. He peered suspiciously at the colorful potions on Orion's belt; he wondered what secrets the bottles contained, and what harm they could cause if he used them. He finally realized why Marco Victor Odious was not the largest current threat and wondered how horrible the others must be if Orion wasn't the greatest threat either.

The next couple of hours would have been arduous for the average person, but they were the easiest hours the group of nine had experienced since they had arrived at the Purple Mountains. Though going down was almost as difficult as going up, over a dozen sorcerers now accompanied them, and they weren't worried about saving their energy for more important matters. Magical stairs, ladders, and clouds like the ones belonging to Watt were constantly appearing as sorcerers helped each other down the cliffs.

Finally, Orion came to a stop and majestically held his hand out to signal for everyone to do the same. His assistants quickly halted and faced him as if they were in the military.

"We have arrived," he said and raised his sword. As if he were tracing a door on the mountainside, he slashed his sword in a rectangular motion. However, after he was done, he had left no mark on the rock. He smiled broadly, and Justin looked at him like he had just announced that he had decided to start a chinchilla farm in northern France.

But, a few seconds later, a door appeared right where he had traced it! Even Hermes looked impressed by the difficult magic Orion had used to hide the door. Orion opened the door with a doorknob that emerged shortly after the entryway had appeared and led them into a tall, wide, and domed room that looked like it had been carved into the mountain. Bronze bricks lined the floors, and the smooth rock walls held burning torches.

"Whoever the architect of this place was, they surely received a promotion," Justin said sarcastically, but everyone was too busy marveling at the bizarre and yet beautiful dome to hear.

Laying on the base of the large dome were sleeping bags, not unlike the tents that Hermes had made. A few of Orion's henchmen sat down on their sleeping bags, yawning. Others kept standing and simply stared at the group of nine with glassy eyes.

"We will continue tomorrow," Orion said. "My followers and I have been walking for too long today, and need to rest."

Rowena snorted and Teddy and April rolled their eyes at him. Justin let out an exasperated sigh, which would have been considered quite rude, but he and the others had reason; they all agreed that Orion probably had no idea what the word "tired" even meant.

As usual, Orion did not notice, as he was completely focused on himself. "You must rest here too. You may use our extra sleeping bags but do not wander off in the night, or you will find no help from us."

Mumbling to himself, Justin grabbed a sleeping bag and pulled it to a secluded space in an attempt to be alone. Wendy tried striking up a conversation with some of the sorcerers, but some didn't reply, a few pretended to be sleeping, and a couple merely babbled nonsense.

"What's with these poor people?" Wendy asked Hermes as she joined back with him and the others as they were gathering up sleeping bags. "If I didn't know better, I'd say they were cursed or something."

"You're forgetting who their leader is," Hermes said with a grave smile. He nodded his head towards Orion. "Yes, I do not have proof, but I believe he has hypnotized some if not most of them. Do you see those bottles on his belt? The green ones are poison, the blue ones are sleeping potions, the yellow ones are healing potions, the red ones are bomb potions, and the purple ones... they're hypnotizing potions. I'd recognize the potion itself anywhere and I assumed that his followers were so loyal to him because of it, but the council would never believe me back when he was Lord Orion because apart from their glassy-eyed stare, his followers bear no proof of hypnotization. Some of them are just supporters of his; some of his acts as lord were positive, after all, and some of his acts struck as positive to some of the sorcerer community but negative to others. His rash decisions will be morally questionable by the sorcerers of today and the magical historians of the future. So, Wendy, I wouldn't attempt to talk to them, even the ones that are right in mind... you may find that you have some moral disagreements with them."

Wendy gulped. "Sounds like politics for non-magic people," she said.

"We may be sorcerers, but we are still only human," the sorcerer responded sagely. "Now, get some sleep."

She nodded and scrambled into a sleeping bag next to Rowena, Grace, and April.

"Hermes, I have something to tell you!" Teddy whispered frantically as Orion somehow began to dim the torches until they eventually went out.

"I'm sorry, it must wait until morning, my child," he responded. "Any further conversation will lead to suspicion by Orion and our mission would be doomed if he thought that we are plotting against him. There would be no escape from this dome, and though Orion's wand was passed onto another sorcerer after he was banished by the Sorcerer Council, he still has his magically engineered sword, potions, and his squad of hypnotized sorcerers that will do as he commands."

And though Teddy tried to further warn him, he was silenced by a spell from the Thunder Crystal.

Unable to talk, he defeatedly climbed into his sleeping bag. He worried like never before, for now, it was not just possible that Marco Victor Odious would slaughter them in their sleep; it was likely. He was so desperate, he even tried sending telepathic messages to Hermes which simply ended in a headache.

He did not sleep a wink that night, due to disconcertment and the fact that the day's walk had lacked the torture of the walks of the weeks before, making him restless. But, the worst part of it all was that he knew there was nothing he could do. A few of the sorcerers took shifts as watch guards and patrolled around the dome, and Teddy was sure that Orion would be alerted if he was found up and about by one of them.

Morning rose with Titus Orion; once he had awoken, the torches magically relit, which annoyed anyone who was still trying to catch a few winks.

After a few minutes of yawning and grumbling, Orion walked to the center of the large room and opened up a trapdoor that no one would have noticed otherwise. He reached into the hidden room and pulled out cans of vegetables among other lousy excuses for a meal.

As Rowena, Grace, April, Watt, Fade, Justin, and Wendy walked over to eat the pitiful breakfast, Teddy ran over to Hermes in a panic.

"There's something I must tell you, and I have to do it now!" Teddy said in a rush.

"My goodness, are you alright Teddy?" Hermes asked with concern in his eyes. "Is this related to the thing you wanted to tell me the previous night?"

Teddy didn't even bother to clarify and started explaining right away.

"Hermes, Orion sent out one of his followers to find Marco Victor Odious and bring him here!" Teddy said frantically without breathing. "I saw him explain it to him yesterday!"

Hermes turned as pale as a snowy owl on a frigid winter morning. "Are you certain of this?"

"Yes!" Teddy yelled, which drew Orion's suspicion. He cautiously approached and began eavesdropping.

Hermes thought this over.

"If what you say is true, I do not think that he will succeed," he decided. "Marco Victor Odious is one of the many enemies of Titus Orion. Orion made dozens of enemies when he was lord, as he fought for the glory of sorcerer-kind. Marco Victor Odious was one of his main targets; he has always been a threat to magic people. They have each left their mark on the other over the years... I doubt a friendship will form between them just because of the Thunder Crystal."

"But Hermes, we have to escape!" Teddy persisted. "If Orion's followers do manage to convince him, he'll kill us all!"

"We depend on Orion, Teddy!" Hermes said forcefully. "We cannot abandon him. The passage is our key to escape, which is why we must stay! I apologize for raising my voice, but I cannot change my answer."

Teddy sighed exasperatedly; there was no use convincing Hermes.

"I'm sorry, Teddy," he said gently. "But when your life is on the line, the right decision has to be made. If we abandon

Orion and the passage, we will be directly open to Marco Victor Odious's wrath. Now, please, go get something to eat."

Teddy grunted in response. He reluctantly walked over to the trapdoor and grabbed a can of spinach mindlessly. Somehow, April could sense his distress.

"I know something's wrong," she said to him. "What is it? I know Orion's up to something, but I can't put my finger on it. Do you know?"

Teddy sighed with relief, glad that someone would believe the truth. "I think... no, I know that he is luring Marco Victor Odious to us," he said defiantly.

April gasped in response. "It's too dangerous to be here, in that case. We must gather our belongings and go!"

"I'm glad someone agrees with me, but Hermes won't let us."

April sighed. "Well, I suppose he knows best... but if either of us sees anything fishy, let's alert him no matter what he says."

Teddy thought that this plan had many flaws, but he nodded; April was the only one who would listen to him, anyway.

Oblivious to Teddy, Orion smiled happily. He had eaves-dropped enough to realize that his mission was completely safe; Marco Victor Odious would be approaching soon, and the Thunder Crystal was in his grasp. Once the criminal took Thunder Crystal, he could finally destroy Hermes and the others and be rid of all of the hatred that he thought the sorcerer had expressed to him over the years.

He then clapped his hands to get the attention of the others.

"We will now lead you through the Purple Mountains," he announced grandly. "To the tunnels!"

He walked over to the side of the dome and again carved a door with his sword. A few moments later, a real door appeared in the rock. However, this time it wasn't as shocking or appalling, so Orion's supporters clapped hard to make up for the lack of surprise from the group.

The former lord opened the door, which led into a surprisingly narrow hallway with a floor similarly made of bronze bricks and walls made of rock. It was so thin that they all had to walk single file.

"Our journey will be long and tedious, but it will greatly reward me... er, you, in the end," he said, correcting himself awkwardly. Teddy glanced at Hermes to see if his opinion had changed, and to his relief, he had begun to look suspicious.

Titus Orion led the way, followed by Hermes. Teddy tried to duck behind Hermes, but one of Orion's followers cut him off. He was then allowed to enter, but when April tried to join the line, she too was cut off. Teddy realized their ploy; Orion realized that they knew what he was up to, and was cutting off their communication. He looked back and saw that Grace had been cut in line next. The Orion-worshiping-sorcerer directly behind him glared, raised her wand, and forced his face to point forward.

Minutes turned into hours as they walked. There was little to no sign of any difference; just more hallway, more torches, and more bricks. However, Teddy noticed that the hallway started to widen. It had to be at least eleven feet across then, and stalagmites were positioned here and there. He hypothesized that they must be nearing a cave that opened to the wilderness, which perhaps meant freedom! That way Orion would never be able to attack them!

But Teddy noticed something odd: the stalagmites were not made of traditional limestone or other rock types; they were made of bronze, just like the ground.

All of a sudden, the ground began to rumble! The bricks began to rise in a wall around him, finally rising almost as high as the ceiling! Looking over the walls ahead and behind, he could see that Hermes and April were stuck in similar bronze brick prison cells. Then it dawned on him: the single file line was to make sure that all of them were in position, the stalagmites were marking points instead of natural phenomenons, and the widening of the hallway was so that Orion could easily move through the passage despite the bronze brick cells.

He had been right all along, but that didn't matter anymore. It was a trap!

Ten

Eluding Orion

As Teddy peered over the top of his bronze-brick jail, he saw Orion walk past him and look down the line of newly risen bronze rooms. His plan had worked; all his followers were safe and everyone else trapped.

He clapped his hands loudly, and his comrades jumped into position. Only one stood in between April, Teddy, Justin, and Wendy (as they were not very threatening) while a few guarded Grace and many guarded Hermes and Rowena. A few more guarded Watt and Fade who were in a cell together.

"I shall now journey to the end of this tunnel and find our friends who have hopefully brought Marco Victor Odious," he announced to his henchmen. Then he spoke directly to the prisoners. "Now to the rest of you, I wouldn't bother trying to escape. Hermes, you are the only one I require alive; if you dare to interfere you will be tortured instead. But for the rest of you…

consider it a miracle that I haven't ordered you killed already. Do not try to escape, or that miracle will disappear."

He smiled menacingly and walked down the extraordinarily long hallway in his usual pompous strut. Teddy kept watching him until he was just a speck.

The young boy had completely given up hope. The situation had never seemed more impossible to escape from. Wands and staffs were pointed into Hermes's brick cell so that he could not use his magic in any way. Watt and Fade were experiencing the same. Even worse, Titus Orion was going to fetch Marco Victor Odious which would inevitably lead to his death. He sank to the bottom of his prison in despair.

However, he heard the clearing of a throat. Then, he heard someone knocking on the cell immediately behind him. He stood up straight and peered through the top of the prison. There was a small gap between the walls and the ceiling; large enough to look through, but too small to crawl through, even for his sorcerer friend's pets.

He looked across to April's cell, and she was staring back at him through the top of hers. She pointed to herself, then to him, and finally to the sorcerer guarding them (who stood right in between their two cells). Then, she gestured to the sorcerer's wand and then to Teddy.

Teddy understood the plan and nodded. He knew the chances of it working were low and it could just be floccinaucinihilipili-fication, but it was the only way they would be able to get out and therefore live.

April reached her hand through the top of her cell (for the gap was so small that was all that she could fit through) and slowly reached towards the sorcerer, who was staring into the distance with a vague expression. Carefully, she reached her hand over, making sure to be completely silent, and paused. Then, she tapped the magical person on the back and retracted her hand as quickly as a cobra!

The sorcerer turned around quickly as if she had just been yanked back into existence from the hypnotization. She raised her oak wand and pointed it at April faster than she could get away!

Luckily, thanks to April's planning, Teddy knew what to do. He reached through the gap between the walls and the ceiling and snagged the wand out of her hand!

She whirled around in surprise, but she got her wits back quickly and reached for the wand...

Boom! An electric blue orb zapped out of the oak wand and blasted the sorcerer to the ground. Her eyes darted around in fear, and Teddy realized that he had successfully cast a Stunning Spell!

However, the other sorcerers guarding Hermes were not oblivious to this. They turned around and faced him with anger etched on their faces, for if their prisoners escaped then they would be failing their master. However, Hermes was quick to figure out what was happening. He pointed the Thunder Crystal at the angered sorcerers, and a barrage of magenta-colored fireworks (smaller than the ones he had first shown to Teddy) erupted from the tip of the mystical artifact. They flew at Orion's magical henchmen like heat-seeking missiles and exploded as soon as they touched them! They combusted into hundreds of other pink blasts that flew in every direction, including into

Hermes's cell. They blew down the walls and he rushed out before he could get hit.

"Get down, children!" Hermes cried to Teddy and April just in time for them to duck down as the fireworks blew their brick prisons into pieces that flew into the air and fell on them like bombs. A shield made of light burst from the Thunder Crystal like an umbrella to protect them from the debris.

"Teddy, use your wand to open the other cells to free everyone else!" Hermes yelled over the commotion. "Use the Laser Cut Spell!"

"I don't know how!" Teddy yelled back nervously. "That other spell I cast was just… spontaneous!"

"Don't worry, it's easy!" Hermes responded. "Just envision what you want… in this case, think of a bright laser beam shining out of your wand and piercing through the bronze!"

He directed his staff and shot more fireworks at the incoming sorcerers who had been guarding the others.

"Come on!" Hermes urged.

"You can do it!" April encouraged him.

Teddy sighed and closed his eyes. He knew that if he truly needed to cast a spell spontaneously, he would be able to cast one, but he had no control over what it would do; it could harm Grace, who was in the cell he was currently trying to destroy. He knew that he needed to focus all of his energy to cast the specific spell that he needed. He now realized why Hermes wanted to save his energy for pressing matters, for it took everything in him just to concentrate. But then, he felt a tingling sensation along his arm. He opened his eyes, and a bright red laser was shooting from the tip of the wand and burning into the cell!

He gasped and smiled in awe! He had cast a spell on purpose!

Teddy moved the wand in a rectangular motion until the bricks fell apart and there was a small door for Grace to crawl out of.

"Thanks, Teddy!" she exclaimed. "April, you help defeat those Orion-worshiping sorcerers! Hermes has his hands full at the moment."

Grace took a dagger out of a secret pocket in her plaid sweater and threw it to April. She caught it and ran into the battle. She snuck behind one of the sorcerers trying to disintegrate Hermes Willowlands and stole his wand. He whipped around, but a point of a dagger made him back up in fear. As if by magic, he happened to walk right into a blast from Hermes's staff.

Grace, who was less aggressive and quite nervous in dangerous situations, stayed close to Teddy and helped the others out of their prisons. Together, they quickly freed Rowena, Wendy, and Justin.

"Why did you have to rescue me last?" Justin grumbled.

"Well, in case you hadn't noticed you're the least valuable at the moment!" Teddy replied.

"And because you were the furthest away," April said, although she snickered at Teddy's comment. While he had been freeing the others, April had already blasted three enemies to the ground with her newly acquired wand. Somehow, even though she had just been freed, Rowena had already beaten nine with her dagger.

However, there were still more remaining, and Hermes, April, and Teddy were exhausted from casting so many spells in addition to the fact that the sorcerers kept getting up despite their injuries. Though Hermes was an experienced and powerful sorcerer, he still looked as weak as a newborn kitten; of course, he had just cast many, many Firework Spells, and even Gregor Knotweigh would not have been able to continue.

The ragged-looking sorcerer fell to his knees, and April and Teddy had to help him up to stand. However, they too were tired; they were new to spell-casting and they were young children with less concentration and magical instinct. Teddy now realized that the concentration step of spell conjuring was only the first part; the actual casting of the spell was so tiring that it felt like his life force was being drained. After all, magical artifacts like staffs and wands merely use the energy of the sorcerer casting the spell; that means that the real energy comes from inside, just as a sword is useless without fencing skills or a pencil is useless with the ability to write.

Bright multicolored blasts shot through the air. One hit Justin's leg, and he fell to the ground shrieking.

"Grace, Wendy, help Justin!" Teddy said tiredly as the sorcerers advanced. "Watt, Fade, and Rowena, you guys make sure they don't reach us. We have to push onward!"

No one questioned his sudden leadership due to the dire situation, so instead Grace and Wendy helped Justin to his feet just as Teddy and April were supporting Hermes. They journeyed as fast as Hermes and Justin would allow them to, giving them the odd appearance of two groups in a four-legged race. Rowena picked up a wand and blasted incoming sorcerers with incredible aim.

"Use… a… Boomerang… Curse…" Hermes moaned in a tone of agony and exhaustion. However, it was not just random babble, for Rowena understood what she was to do. She pointed the wand at her dagger and a yellow light like a rope extended out of the magical artifact and wrapped around the weapon. After it was completely covered, the light rope disappeared, but the dagger had a strange yellow glint to it. Rowena threw the enchanted weapon and it sliced through an enemy sorcerer's shoulder, leaving a scar and causing them to yelp and drop their wand in pain. However, after the blade made its mark, it rebounded and flew back into Rowena's hand! She laughed in triumph and continued throwing the enchanted dagger into the cluster of Orion's followers. She threw it in such a way that it did not touch the sorcerers themselves, but near them instead. Yelping in fear, they would jump away from the rebounding dagger. Rowena continued doing this, herding them into the center, and finally, when they were all grouped in a small circle, she retreated and made way for Hermes's two pets.

Fade acted as a distraction, jumping around and turning invisible every now and then. When the magical comrades of Orion looked at Fade and pointed their wands and staffs at her, Watt shot bolts of lightning at them which temporarily stunned and electrified them. However, their powers were unusually faint; because their power came from the Thunder Crystal which came from their master who was worn out and drained of energy, they too were tired and less dominating than before.

Luckily, the majority of the enemy sorcerers were either retreating or lying on the ground in pain, giving the others time to pursue through the tunnel and allowing Rowena and the animals to stop fighting. The shaft continued to widen, and more and more stalagmites grew. Now, the stalagmites were made of rock instead of brick, and some of the bricks were missing which revealed more rock underneath. Teddy sighed with relief; now he was sure that they were getting close.

They could smell the fresh air and feel the wind now. There were no more bronze bricks, only the rock of the cave. Then, at the end of the tunnel, they saw the mountains once again!

Their feet ached, but they knew Orion's followers would be getting back to them soon (spells cast by inexperienced sorcerers seldom last for a long time). Teddy and April pulled the now unconscious Hermes along, now longing to be safe and out in the mountains instead of stuck in the dangerous tunnel...

They heard the clearing of a throat. April and Teddy gasped and pulled Hermes behind a stalagmite. Wendy and Grace instinctively did the same and pulled Justin behind one as well. Watt and Fade feebly joined Hermes. Rowena raised her dagger with a look of interest in her eye, but Grace pulled her behind a stalagmite before she could stupidly challenge the threat.

After a few suspenseful seconds with no further noises, Teddy assumed that the person who was clearing their throat simply had a cold or something and the noise had nothing to do with their presence. He peered out from behind the stalagmites to observe. After nothing appeared to happen, April got enough courage to do the same.

Orion was looking into the distance with his magical spyglass to his eye. From what Teddy could see, the magical engineer had a disgruntled expression on his face.

"Where is that idiot?" he asked himself fiercely. "He should be back by now... he's probably dead, killed by animals or the cold, too bad for him… but I must wait a few more minutes, just in case…"

He was twisting the dial on his spyglass viciously, paying no attention to anything around him. Teddy thought about running up and tackling the madman, but a glance at the scabbard on his belt and the knowledge of what it was holding forced him to stay put.

He heard a shuffling noise, and over his shoulder, he saw Rowena trying to get up to attack Orion and Grace and Wendy holding her back with all of their force. Teddy whipped out his wand and sent a Silencing Spell at her; he knew that she hated waiting in a position of hopelessness (and just waiting for anything in general), but if Orion heard them he would kill them, Marco Victor Odious would get the Thunder Crystal, and the Oracle would destroy the world. Luckily, Orion was so invested in his search that he did not hear them. Teddy also established that he was a bit hard of hearing.

After a couple of minutes, Orion growled and turned away; he had given up. He headed back into the tunnels still muttering to himself.

After waiting to make sure that he was a good distance away, Teddy signaled to April, Wendy, Grace, and Rowena that it was safe to get away. Wendy and Grace supported Justin again, and Hermes, who had regained some of his strength, walked supported by his staff. Teddy and April grabbed Watt and Fade, who would use up Hermes's energy if they stayed active instead. They slowly tiptoed, edging towards the exit…

The sound of a sword being unsheathed made them all nearly jump out of their skin.

"Do you take me to be an idiot?" Orion asked menacingly. "Did you possibly forget that I was holding a spyglass that can see all? But no matter! It looks like you will be easy to destroy..."He glanced towards Hermes limping along and smirked. He raised his sword high in the air.

"I've always felt wands and crystals lack any use... anything that uses my energy for its power is something that I find more of a danger to myself than a weapon that I wield," Orion continued. "You always disagreed with me, Hermes... you said that the greatest power comes from within. Well, look at the difference between us now..." He laughed loudly.

"Don't do this, Orion," Hermes whispered feebly. Slowly but surely, he was regaining energy. "You have no idea what is going on... if you kill me, the Oracle would return."

Orion didn't even stutter. "Explain how that is possible," he laughed. "I'm not stupid enough to unleash that beastly creature. I suppose you think that because you have that monster trapped in your crystal, you have the power to stop me from taking it... well, the only thing special about that crystal is its history!"

"Marco Victor Odious will capture the Thunder Crystal," Hermes said defiantly. "What did you think he was doing here, having a tea party with his followers? No, that's what you're doing."

Hermes smiled. The Thunder Crystal sparked. He stood up a little taller. If he could buy enough time, he could trap Orion using his magic.

Orion growled deeply and approached them with his sword drawn.

"He will rob the Thunder Crystal from you if you kill me," Hermes continued. Teddy and the others held their breath as Orion approached. "I'm sorry that I made you feel this horrible on the Sorcerer Council, but your ideas were and still are mad. Don't be a fool, Ori…"

The madman threw a bright green bottle at Hermes, who was too stunned to move! Teddy lunged towards him and spontaneously cast a Bomb Spell. When the spell hit the bottle, it exploded, and shards of glass and poison alike flew through the air, thankfully avoiding Hermes or anyone else.

Orion swung his sword, blinded by rage at his foe. The blade pierced through the rock that it hit and left a strange purple stain wherever it touched. A few moments after contact, the substance began eating away at its targets, eventually disintegrating them.

Rowena grabbed her dagger and threw it with all of her might, but Orion blocked it with a mad swing of his sword. Instead of rebounding, it fell to the ground covered in the purple stain.

Grace hopped behind a stalagmite, leaving the injured Justin out in the open next to the pure chaos. Wendy was quick to help him out of the way, but Orion, still oscillating his sword insanely through the air, started moving dangerously close to them.

To protect his cousins, Teddy sent a Stunning Spell at Orion. However, his sword blocked the latest attack. Hermes quickly created a strange tan-colored and seemingly useless blast that shot into the ground. A small plant began to sprout from the rock where it had hit, but that was the least of their concerns.

Because Hermes's attack proved ineffective (seemingly), April jumped into action by helping Teddy try to stun the ballistic

Orion. One blast hit him directly in the eyes, but he was so powerful that all it did was impair his vision. However, this was not an improvement, as it seemed to only make him more wild and aggressive with his swings.

Rowena (pushing Grace out of the way for her act of cowardice) grabbed Justin and together she and Wendy pulled him out of the way just before Orion's sword would have struck him.

Meanwhile, though Hermes was quickly losing energy, his power seemed to transfer to the plant that grew as Orion continued to fight. The plant seemed to be turning into a tree, a willow to be exact, just like the one in front of Teddy's house.

When it finally grew to a height of around six feet, the peaceful sorcerer closed his eyes. From that moment, he controlled the tree's every movement. Though it could not walk, it punched, grabbed, and struck the greatly angered Orion as he searched blindly for the man who once disrespected him and caused his position of power to be destroyed.

Orion figured out where Teddy's and April's shots were coming from and charged towards them. They gasped and tried to walk backwards away from him, but they only tripped...

Orion's sword was knocked out of his hand as the magical willow tree grabbed him and held him closely to its trunk! It was now much taller and stronger, and without his sword he could not fight it. Hermes opened his eyes, and the tree stopped moving, although it stayed in the same position pinning Orion to its trunk.

"Everyone, we must go!" he shouted. He and his pets feebly hobbled along out of the cave, and everyone followed. Justin was now being supported by Wendy and Rowena instead of Grace, as Rowena would not allow her to after she abandoned him to rescue herself.

"I will get you for this, Hermes!" Orion yelled. "I will have my revenge! You will regret ever challenging me! Ever!"

They knew that his followers would be coming soon due to the fact that they were probably awakening from the stunning and firework spells and because of Orion's volume, but they didn't have time to do anything about it. They needed to find shelter fast, for the sun was setting and the temperature dropping.

Immediately, Teddy regretted wishing to feel the fresh air and wind. It froze and stung him with its power and whipped his hair in his face.

Still, they had to persist. They passed multiple caves, but they all agreed (except Justin who just wished to sleep, even though he didn't even have to walk by himself) that they were too close to Orion's passage. Finally, half an hour later, they settled on a fairly large cave just as the moon rose into the sky and the sun dipped below the horizon.

Shivering and exhausted, they stepped into the smooth cave. Wendy collapsed from having to drag Justin along, and Justin himself was already fast asleep; though he had not worked nearly as hard as the others, all of his angry muttering must have tired him out.

Hermes was about to make the tents, but Teddy insisted that he should save his energy; after all, he was very drowsy and drained after so much spell-casting along with all of the walking they had done that day. And so he instead simply curled up on the ground and attempted to sleep peacefully.

Rowena made sure that her daughter was okay before allowing her to sleep, and she did the same to Teddy; it was the first time she had acted motherly towards him, and he was surprised. He thought that Grace was more of the kind of person to do such things, but she was already asleep.

Rowena checked the cave before she hit the hay, and so Teddy lay on the cold ground, finally ready to doze off after the long day…

A loud roaring sound shook him awake and practically shook his whole body! At the back of the cave was a creature that they had not seen in the darkness, a massive animal that had remained hidden until Rowena accidentally woke her up.

A grizzly bear appeared from the shadows, and Rowena had to run backwards to avoid its claws. Everyone was now awake, and stared at the bear in horror. Hermes grabbed his staff and held it out in front to threaten the bear; he knew that he was too weak and the bear strong enough to harm them seriously, but he thought that perhaps it might scare her. Teddy agreed; he had always heard that if you see a bear in the wild your best chance of survival was to scare it.

However, the staff seemed to only make it more angry. It stood up on its hind legs and roared loudly. She was taller than all of them, even Rowena. Teddy could hear his cousins screaming loudly, and he let out a small whimper of worry. Even calm and intelligent April looked as if she were about to fall into an active volcano.

The grizzly bear lunged at them and struck the staff out of Hermes's hands! April and Rowena reached for their own wands, but they were stuck on the other side of the cave behind the mammoth creature!

Then, Teddy saw why the bear wasn't retreating. Two cubs peered their heads out from behind their fearsome mother. He had watched enough nature shows to know that messing with a mother grizzly bear's cubs will cost you your life.

"Run!" he shouted to the others. "Rowena, don't stay and fight! Everyone, get out!"

Once again, no one questioned him. Rowena reluctantly grabbed Justin and pulled him towards the mouth of the cave, and April picked up Watt and Fade, grunting from their combined weight. Hermes realized that there was no way that everyone could get away from the mammoth creature safely; she was enormous and quick-witted.

Hermes gathered his last bit of energy and lunged for his staff! He grabbed it and the Thunder Crystal shone bright. This action seemed to aggravate the grizzly bear even more, as Hermes was extremely near her cubs.

Hermes closed his eyes and created an invisible wall between them. The bear tried to swipe her enormous paw through it, but the paw stopped as if it was touching extraordinarily clear glass. However, she rammed her entire body against the barrier, and she was so enormous and heavy that the barrier started to break with a strange crackling noise!

Teddy instinctively grabbed his wand for a spell for another wall. With their combined shield, the bear could not get through. She roared and clawed, but none of her attacks made it through the shield, and Rowena, Justin, Wendy, Grace, and April carrying both of the pets managed to run out unscathed. Although

Teddy had grown to admire his new wand, he knew he needed to sacrifice it to save them, and so he created a hole in the shield and threw the wand into the blocked part of the cave. The bear went berserk and dove for the wand and so Hermes and Teddy retreated. The shield was destroyed, but Teddy bought them just enough time to run away without being clawed or pummeled to the ground. They could still hear her roaring, so everyone quickened their pace, Rowena now dragging Justin which cut his face a bit and made him yell in pain. However, it helped them speed up their escape, so Rowena did not slow down.

Finally, they reached another cave, this one much smaller so they could see that it was bear-free. April dropped the pets on the floor and Rowena put down Justin whose face was now scratched up along with his leg from being dragged so much. And without bothering to do anything else, Teddy and the others dropped like stones; after a madman and a bear, there was nothing that would keep them awake, even the gorgeous northern lights shining down on them, flickering with brilliant shades of blue and green and flowing across the sky like a mystical serpent.

Eleven

Purple Mountain Pandemonium

Surprisingly, rain and not snow poured down on the roof of the small cavern. The sound of the droplets echoing through the open space jerked Teddy awake, and, after realizing that it was practically noon, he abandoned his sleep and rose to his feet.

Justin, Wendy, April, and Grace were still sleeping (as usual), and so were Watt, Fade, and Rowena (which was not as usual). However, despite the bags under his eyes, Hermes was awake and still. He had not bothered to make a fire, because he wished to take a long break from using magic, and also because the inside of the diminutive cavern was nearly as damp as the outside.

Teddy realized that they were at a much lower altitude than they thought if it was raining. The group had to have dropped a great amount of altitude walking through the path under the mountains. Teddy also realized with surprise that it was May now. With sadness, he thought of the time he had missed with his family, and (with slightly less sadness) how much school he had missed. He missed electricity, basic appliances, his friends, and free meals whenever he pleased, but what he missed most was the feeling of comfort that one has in their own home in their own bed. He remembered how the enormous willow tree had swayed in the Alaskan wind just outside of his room, stationed next to his bed like a guard.

He stood up, but immediately regretted it; he was still sore and bruised from the previous night, in addition to being drained of magical and physical energy. So, instead, he sat down again and listened to the noisy pounding of rain.

He felt weak and alone. Hermes had not said good morning, for the sorcerer himself was exhausted; the only reason he was awake was to keep watch.

However, Hermes should have been keeping a better look-out, for not one, not two, but three figures stood outside of the cave.

Dylan McCamel, Michelle Laurens, and Shannon Jones stood hidden in the pine trees surrounding the petite hideout, freezing and soaked to the bone; though it was warm enough for rain to pour down instead of snow, it was only a few degrees above freezing.

The bandits shivered, longing to be in the cozy cave, but they knew that the enemy was in there. The three of them had watched the group of nine since they had escaped from Orion's red-haired follower. The red-haired man was a sorcerer, but the bandits had the element of surprise, and attacked him while he was muttering to himself about where Marco Victor Odious was. After all, they could not trust Orion or any of his brainwashed comrades, not after what he had done to their master. They tied the magical man to a pine tree higher up in the mountains so he would not be able to alert Orion of anything.

The bandits had watched Hermes and the others fight Orion and defeat him and then foolishly wander into a mother bear's cave. They had watched them run down the mountain and collapse into sleep. And now, they had them under surveillance, and they were trapped. There may have been more of them than the bandits, but the miscreants knew that one of the occupants of the cave was on their side. One of the members of the moral side was not moral. One of them was in cahoots with Marco Victor Odious, as the bandits were, for their master had finally told them who had freed them from prison. All they had to do was wait and the Thunder Crystal would be in their grasp to hand over to their master. Then and only then would they be safe from that wretched, evil man who commanded them.

Of course, the travelers had no way of knowing about Marco Victor Odious's malicious plans, especially since most of them (including the spy) were asleep.

However, as the day went on and the rain died down, Teddy's cousins and the others began to wake up.

And after waking up, the first thing that Wendy did was go straight to Hermes.

"I demand you bring us home at once!" she shouted. She was scratched and aching from the night before in addition to being generally steamed. "You have forced us away from our homes against our will, and I refuse to stay out here any longer!"

Teddy had never seen her that mad, not even towards him. He looked worriedly at Hermes, to see his reaction. Luckily, the sorcerer did not look angry; in fact, his eyes looked quite sorrowful. He lowered his head.

"I am terribly sorry, Wendy, and the rest of you, too," he began. "I know I have put you all in danger, but believe me, you would have been in greater danger if I had let you stay put at Teddy's house. However, I believe you are right... it is time for you to go home. The danger has passed and since we took Orion's path under the Purple Mountains, Marco Victor Odious and his bandits are probably lost looking for us at the top of the peaks!"

He chuckled to himself and smiled. Wendy smiled too. Teddy couldn't believe his ears. He was finally going to go home and his misery would finally come to an end! But Hermes was a foolish man to say this, as their trouble had barely begun.

A grunting sound signaled the awakening of Justin. Teddy, grinning from ear to ear, wished to tell him the good news immediately, but he decided to wait until Justin had woken up a little more.

Justin's waking reaction was similar to Wendy's; as soon as he realized where he was, he jumped up and began yelling...except he targeted his anger at everyone.

"This is madness!" he yelled. "You stupid wizard, fix this immediately! Put things back the way they were!"

"I can't do that, but we are taking you back..." Hermes started calmly, but Teddy interrupted him. All of his giddiness washed away at Justin's statement. He thought, why wouldn't Justin ever pay attention to the sorcerer? Why wouldn't he learn?

"He is a sorcerer, not a wizard, won't you ever listen?" Teddy shot back. Teddy had really angered him now. Justin turned to him.

"This is all your fault, pest!" Justin shouted. "If you hadn't been obsessed with those lame magical animals, this never would have happened!"

"Now really, that's enough!" Wendy said before Teddy could reply. "Stop arguing at once!"

"Don't you agree with me?" Justin asked her. "This adventure has been awful! But if you want to turn against me, then so be it!"

He went to push Wendy to the ground, but she merely stepped away, and Justin tripped over due to his limp.

Now they were all arguing, and Justin screamed in agony and yelled at her and the rest of them so insultingly and so loudly that even the hidden bandits jumped.

"All of you, behave, now!" Rowena yelled. Grace urged her to stop and let the children sort the argument out themselves, but her cousin had already extracted her dagger.

She pointed it threateningly towards Justin, then Wendy, then Teddy, and then her daughter. "Silence, all of you, this behavior is unacceptable!" she bellowed. "There is serious work to be done, killers seeking us out!"

The three bandits looked at each other worriedly. Would she give them away?

"You're to blame too!" Justin yelled at her. Wendy silently pleaded for him to stop, but he continued. "You think that the world revolves around your own problems! Well, what about mine? What about my hunger and my pain? You're blind to our suffering!"

Rowena was furious and red in the face.

"Rowena, please, I need to talk to you," Grace finally said. She walked over from her spot next to the worried and fearful Hermes and pulled her into the forest.

The children's squabble continued, continually getting more and more intense and physical. Everyone complained and yelled about how the others were to blame, but Justin was the noisiest still. Once it reached a certain point of physicality and Teddy and April realized that someone would truly get hurt, they tried to stop the others before someone did get injured, but their efforts only seemed to anger the other two even more. Wendy was not as aggressive as Justin, but she too was sore, irritable, and homesick.

Hermes, too kindly and polite to get involved, continued to watch from a distance sadly. Though he may have been able to help using his wisdom and calm nature, he simply despised fights, everything about them. But, he could not bear to take his eyes off of them; if something bad happened, his magic would be needed.

However, out of the corner of his eye, he noticed something strange. He finally decided to look away from the increasing chaos, and so he looked around the cave, scanning for the odd thing that he had seen a moment ago.

He gasped. His staff was in its normal position next to him, but there was no Thunder Crystal on top of it! It had been stolen!

He looked around wildly as the shouting grew. He noticed something else; Rowena and Grace had been visible moments before in the trees, but they were gone now.

That is when he realized that he was wrong. They were still in terrible danger, and everyone needed to gather inside of the cave instantly.

But, before he could act, a high-pitched scream rang out! Everything stopped, including the arguing. Everyone turned to the forest in fear. Even Justin had a look of terror on his face.

Hermes ran into the woodland swiftly. The adolescents were so surprised that they followed suit.

Another scream rang out, and they dashed through the pine trees to find the person in trouble. Finally, they found Grace, looking petrified and distraught.

"Grace!" Hermes yelled. "What is going on? Why did you scream?"

"Where's Mom?" April asked with a panic.

Grace began stuttering, but she was too overwhelmed to continue. Hermes put an arm around her. "Breathe," he told her.

Grace slowly breathed in and out. Then she spoke.

"I grabbed Rowena to calm her down, and pulled her into the woods after she threatened you four with her dagger," she gasped. "I began talking to her to calm her down, telling her that it was not her place to get involved with your argument. But... something seemed strange about her. She was more angry than I had ever seen her and yet... happy. And she kept reaching into her pocket. It seemed sort of lumpy, and I didn't know why... until now."

She gulped and continued her story. "She stormed off into the woods. I thought she was just mad, but… I think she wanted me to follow her because when I raced after her, I saw them!"

She gasped loudly and looked around as if the "them" that she was referring to would jump out at her and cut her to bits.

"Who?" Hermes asked. "Who did you see?" Everyone leaned in, eager to hear.

However, Grace did not answer this question. Instead, she simply continued with her tale. "They… they saw me and grabbed me and shoved me to the ground! That's why I screamed. Rowena pulled out the Thunder Crystal from her pocket and handed it to them! Then, they ran off into the mountains together!"

Grace began sobbing in fear. Hermes looked at her, with both worry and sadness in his eyes.

"Who were they?" he asked, already knowing the answer.

Grace swallowed and said two words that would make them all realize that their current anger and personal troubles were small potatoes.

"The bandits!"

Twelve

Battle of the Bandits

It would have normally taken them a long, long time to reach the edge of the Purple Mountains without Orion's passageway, but Hermes, Teddy, Justin, Wendy, Grace, and the two immortal pets made it to the beginning of White Pine Forest (a small forest that fed into Metronome Woodland) in just a week. They were fueled by adrenaline to reach Teddy's village before the bandits did so they could save the world. Avoiding Marco Victor Odious was the least of their problems, for the Thunder Crystal had already been stolen and he would not need anything more from them.

Hermes would have messaged Nightwhale Castle to inform them of the robbery, but he had no magical artifact to send a message. In addition to this, they had lost Rowena, whose expert hunting skills gave them food and protection. Grace, who was more of an indoor person and did not even know how to throw or catch a ball, let alone make a fishing rod or set a trap, proved to be completely useless compared to her cousin. They relied on Teddy for those sorts of things from then on. He did learn a few survival tips from his time as a boy scout, but he too was practically helpless in comparison to the hero-turned-villain Rowena.

Luckily, the group still had the magical powers of Watt and Fade on their side. However, their powers became increasingly frail since the Thunder Crystal was being taken further and further away. The bandits were progressing even faster than they were, due to the worry of upsetting their despicable master; Marco Victor Odious wished for the Thunder Crystal immediately. The next Dark Moon was approaching, and the Oracle could only be released from her Interdiction Curse in the place where she had been forced into the said portal: the village where Teddy lived.

So, the comparatively moral side of the conflict persisted to catch up to the comparatively villainous side of the conflict. The temperatures were rising every day and the snow was melting away. The Purple Mountains (which began to look small in the distance) began to lose their signature purple tint, looking blue and gray instead. White Pine Forest looked olive green and was no longer covered in powder blue ice and brilliant white snow. The aurora borealis seldom lit up the night with its magical twisting and twirling anymore, and no snow storms bothered the sorcerer and the non-magic people he was assigned to escort.

After exiting the protection of the Purple Mountains (which were so massive that they were unlikely to run into anyone unexpectedly), Teddy fashioned makeshift spears for everyone made of long sticks whose points had been sharpened so much that they could even match Rowena's dagger (although not wielded by Rowena herself, because that would be terrifying, and even April could not gather enough strength from her sadness of how her mother turned to the dark side of the battle to fight her). In addition to protecting them, the spears also made reasonable hunting weapons.

However, despite the new multipurpose spears, Teddy, April, Hermes, and Grace had inklings of fear slide through them with each step they took. If they did not make it to the village in time, war would erupt between the Oracle and the rest of the world, and the only people who could defeat her would be the sorcerers who were already few. Justin and Wendy were not afraid, for they did not understand; they assumed that the Oracle would simply kill all of the remaining sorcerers and leave the rest of the planet alone. This was ridiculous, but they could not realize the truth because of their simple lack of imagination; they could not imagine what an evil creature the Oracle was, and they could not imagine anything horrible ever happening to them. This was the same reason why they could not even cast simple spells, even with a magical artifact such as Hermes's crystal or a wand in their hands.

Every night, at least one of them stayed up (usually Hermes or Grace to spare the children from exhaustion) to keep guard. Along with tents, Hermes also created a series of invisible barriers around their campsite (there were no longer caves to sleep in since they had exited the mountains). Every crunch of the leaves or the snap of branches was one of the criminals to them, and Teddy almost gave up sleeping every night, finding it easier to stay awake in the companionable comfort of the others.

Still, every day they were getting closer to the lone Alaskan village, closer to the Thunder Crystal, closer to their victory. Then, Teddy thought, his life would finally be back to normal. But somehow, this made him even more sorrowful. A question loomed in his mind, waiting to be asked, wishing to be answered. Finally, one night, he could not keep it in any longer.

"Hermes?" Teddy asked his sorcerer friend.

"Yes, my child?"

"I was just wondering… you know, most people don't know about magic, right?"

"That is correct."

"Well, now that I do know… is there any way I can become a sorcerer?"

Hermes sighed. This worried Teddy. "I do not know, Teddy," the sorcerer said. "I don't want you to give up your life for sorcery… we usually don't recruit people of completely non-magic families…"

"Recruit?" Teddy asked.

"Yes, recruit," he explained. "As you know, there are multiple sorcery occupations, such as magical engineering, magical philosophy, and of course a position on the Sorcerer Council, although that is only for well-trained magical folk. Anyway, one of those jobs is sorcerer recruiting… my good friend Daffodil Coolwater on the Sorcerer Council works as a recruiter as a side job, in fact. Recruiters seek either orphans who have no true family or (and this is more common) people who are partially descended from sorcerers, although without knowledge of it. They could be dangerous to the non-magical people around them, so recruiters bring them to sorcerers who are available to take apprentices."

"Sort of like how you 'brought' me on this crazy adventure?" Teddy asked.

"Well, yes," Hermes admitted. "Magic is one of the most dangerous forces on the planet… It is unpredictable and unique. So, sorcerers must be a bit forceful in situations as such."

He then continued. "An apprentice would choose their magical name when they complete their training (mine is Hermes Willowlands, of course), and they can leave their teacher and enter the world. They can still have non-magical occupations, but they would no longer be dangerous to the world around them, for if they found a magical artifact without knowing of their powers, they could cause chaos without even knowing it."

Teddy thought about this. "I still don't see why I can't get recruited and trained by a sorcerer."

"Well, I'm no sorcerer recruiter, but someday I could take you to one to see if you're descended from a magical bloodline, as you're not an orphan, of course," Hermes responded. "You know, when all of this havoc is over."

Teddy smiled at this; it was a possibility. However, he had one more question.

"Hermes?"

"Yes?"

"What's your name? Your birth name, I mean."

He smiled slightly. "Well, we're not supposed to tell anyone, but… I was called Jack Butterworth."

Teddy grinned. He didn't tell Hermes, but he did not blame him for choosing a completely different name, even if it was a totally weird name like Hermes Willowlands.

With the thought of a future of magic, Teddy finally got a good night's sleep. This was lucky, for he needed it for the treacherous battle that lay just ahead of them in the woodland.

By noon the next day, they had reached the edge of White Pine Forest and crossed into Metronome Woodland. Their hopes were rising tremendously; the Dark Moon was multiple days away which left time for them to reach the village! However, danger still loomed ahead, and the closer they got to the village, the more anxious they became.

A cold wind as sharp as a blade blew at their hair and Hermes's long robe. A chill ran through them all, a chill unrelated to (although not helped by) the icy gusts.

Hermes stopped. "I sense something… dangerous," he said.

"What do you mean, sense?" Justin asked rudely.

Hermes did not respond verbally, instead gesturing to Watt and Fade. They were frozen in mid-step, and Teddy realized that Hermes had probably stopped at the sight of this. Fade's ears pointed backward and the fur on her back was raised, and Watt was bearing his teeth and his tail was anything but wagging.

Wendy gulped and started whirling around, searching for the cause of danger. April looked around too, but she looked up instead at the branches of the trees.

Suddenly, she gasped, and a loud snap rang out!

Three figures who had been hiding in the branches jumped down, encircling the group. Each was wearing a cloak: one in a yellow cloak, one in a plum cloak, and one in a red cloak. It was the bandits.

They smirked at their victims, pleased to be giving off such a fearful vibe. Then, when Hermes looked away, he could not find his faithful pets! Somehow, they had disappeared while everyone was looking at the bandits!

There was a frightened silence, until April spoke.

"Where is my mother?" she demanded. "What have you done with her?"

"Oh, foolish girl, didn't you know?" Michelle Laurens asked mockingly. "Your mother is on our side."

"You'll never be as frightening as Marco Victor Odious," April said menacingly. Her very tone made even Teddy fearful. "You're only his accomplices." The bandits growled. They were enraged, for they knew it was true.

"Please be quiet, April," Grace whispered to her, but April seemed to take no notice.

"My mother is not a murderer, she's not a criminal!" April shouted. "She would never do... what Marco Victor Odious did to my father."

The three bandits looked at each other, eyebrows raised. Then they glared at her once more.

"You idiot child, your dad isn't dead!" Shannon Jones smirked. "No, he's in a much worse condition..."

April gasped. Teddy was extremely taken aback as well. The father of April Finnegan was still alive?

April immediately began firing questions rapidly and anxiously at the misdemeanants. "Where is he? Why hasn't he returned? What has become of him?"

"We're in no position to tell you that," Dylan McCamel said fiercely. "Marco Victor Odious ordered us to capture you, and we shall follow his orders!"

However, despite the fierce voice and the glare, Teddy sensed fear in Dylan McCamel, as well as the rest of the bandits. He felt an advantage over them; besides, they did not appear to wield any weapons.

Unfortunately, Teddy's second assumption was incorrect. Dylan McCamel reached deep into a hidden pocket in his cloak and pulled out a hatchet, crooked and sharp. Michelle Laurens grabbed her belt and produced a machete, such as one might see in an expensive jungle-themed action movie filled with large CGI animals that bear absolutely no resemblance to the real things. Finally, Shannon Jones reached behind her back and, having done track and field in high school, pulled out a spear fashioned like a javelin, but so sharp that it made Teddy's hand-crafted spears look like toothpicks.

"I advise you to drop your weapons," Shannon Jones snarled with a smirk. "That way, you won't suffer as awfully."

Grace slowly lowered hers to the ground. Justin whimpered and dropped his as well. Wendy looked torn between holding and dropping hers.

Luckily, Hermes, April, and of course Teddy kept their hands tight on their weapons. The bandits smirked at the sight of them: a sorcerer without any way to harness his magical power and two children.

Shannon Jones smiled. "I suppose you will have to suffer, then… more than you would have, at least."

All of a sudden, the three bandits lunged at their prey! Michelle Laurens sliced April's spear in half with her machete and it fell to the ground in pieces. Shannon Jones jumped at Hermes, who attempted to block her attack, but was sent tumbling to the ground with a spin of her javelin. However, when Dylan McCamel attempted to do the same to Teddy, great shock came to all of them, bandits and heroes alike, for Wendy lunged herself at the miscreant and knocked the hatchet out of his hand. The axe-like weapon flew through the air and lodged itself into a tree trunk and Dylan McCamel himself tripped over his cloak and fell to the ground.

Teddy looked gratefully at his cousin, but there was no time to say thank-you, for having disarmed April and Hermes, the other bandits directed their attention to the cousins. Unfortunately for them, Hermes was quick and sharp-minded and grabbed his spear calmly but speedily and knocked Michelle Laurens to the dirt. She toppled into Dylan McCamel, which greatly increased his struggle to get up.

Shannon Jones, more competent than the other two, growled. "Get up, your imbeciles!" she hissed. "Dylan, Michelle, time for Plan B!"

While Shannon Jones fended off Hermes, Teddy, and Wendy (who still had their wooden spears), Dylan McCamel and Michelle Laurens sneakily stood up and ran over to their weapons. Dylan grabbed his hatchet (with much difficulty, as it was lodged deeply in the tree it had been launched into), Michelle Laurens picked up her knife, and then together they ran over to particularly large trees with thick trunks and began chopping them down.

Meanwhile, Hermes, Teddy, and Wendy were beating the other bandit brutally. She may have had more skill and a better weapon than them, but the sorcerer and his young comrades had strength in numbers, especially after April grabbed Grace's dropped spear and pricked the criminal in the back. Cowardly and weaponless Grace hid behind a tree, but Justin on the other hand picked up his own spear and joined in the fun.

Shannon Jones was now clearly outnumbered. She was scratched, scraped, and worried, her eyes now full of fear. However, a distant sound washed away her worry. Hermes, Teddy, Wendy, April, and Justin turned around in surprise as they heard a loud crackling sound. Shannon Jones grinned at their surprise and ducked away.

Suddenly, an enormous tree toppled over! April, Teddy, and the latter's two cousins jumped out of the way just in time, but Hermes was not so lucky. It fell directly on the poor sorcerer, knocking the wind out of him and trapping him under its wide trunk! Dylan McCamel smiled and ran towards Hermes with his hatchet raised.

"Run!" he yelled to Teddy and the others. However, when a second tree fell over, Teddy was not quick enough; Michelle Laurens used her machete to aim the tree before it fell, making it knock into the young boy! She ran over to Teddy with her weapon raised just as Dylan McCamel was about to reach Hermes!

But then, a lightning bolt struck Dylan McCamel square in the chest! He fell over and his hatchet went flying once again. Fade ran over and caught the weapon with her mouth and brought it over to Hermes, who began chopping himself free.

However, the lightning-struck bandit staggered up with a glint of pure anger in his eyes. Watt's lightning was much weaker due to the Thunder Crystal becoming increasingly farther away. Fade's magical abilities were also lessened, and she now became only semi-transparent instead of completely invisible. However, her claws did not rely on the Thunder Crystal to work, and so the Bengal cat launched herself onto Dylan McCamel, scratching and scraping him so Hermes could free himself.

Unfortunately, Watt and Fade were too distracted by their master's peril to realize Teddy's! He too was still trapped with an angry bandit running towards him. April ran over to help, but she had forgotten about Shannon Jones. From a great distance away, the intelligent bandit threw her javelin at poor April. Luckily, it did not hit her directly, but it scraped her leg and she fell to the ground, bleeding terribly. Shannon Jones smiled, and Michelle Laurens grinned maliciously as she got closer and closer to her victim...

Justin jumped at Michelle Laurens and speared her with his stick! Teddy was shocked that his useless and obnoxious cousin had done such a thing; Wendy he could see, but for Justin... Well, Teddy considered seeing it to be a once-in-a-lifetime experience.

While Justin continued aggressively hitting Michelle Laurens, Wendy ran over and helped Teddy out from under the tree. Simultaneously, Hermes had also been freed by Watt. Grace (seeing no huge danger remaining) speed-walked over to her niece and helped her to her feet.

Justin and Fade finally ceased their attacks, seeing that the bandits were scratched and beaten badly. Hermes pulled them over to a tree, and Watt created a rope made out of electrical material. All seemed well as Teddy rose from his trapped position.

"Thanks," he muttered to Wendy and Justin.

"Teddy, you were going to die!" Wendy scolded him. "Be more careful next time!"

"Don't expect that from me again," Justin said sternly. "That was a one time thing."

Teddy sighed at his cousins' foolishness. "Justin, I don't think that's the last fighting you'll have to do. And Wendy, I'm not the one who needs to be protected in this war. If I'm killed, we will still win."

Wendy sighed. "Teddy, we just saved your life."

"Well, I did say thanks, didn't I?" Teddy said with a laugh. Wendy laughed as well, and surprisingly, so did Justin.

However, their laughter was interrupted when a javelin flew through the air!

"Get down!" Teddy yelled to his cousins. They did so, and the spear flew just above their heads and into the bracken!

Hermes, having finished imprisoning Dylan McCamel and Michelle Laurens, turned around and saw the third bandit running away, her long ponytail whizzing behind her. He chased after her with incredible speed, even with his long robe.

Shannon Jones was unarmed, but she was a fast runner. But, she should have remembered that Hermes's pets were still in the mix. Watt turned into a lightning bolt and zapped through the air, while Fade invisibly leaped ahead.

The third bandit, unaware of the pets, continued running. Smiling, she knew that she would keep running until she lured

Hermes Willowlands into a trap. But then, Fade appeared out of nowhere (having been invisible) and leaped at her! Watt (in lightning bolt form) zapped her in the back and transformed back into the adorable beagle he was. Shannon Jones groaned and dropped to the forest floor. Watt and Fade dragged her back to the others, and Watt conjured up another rope to tie her with her fellows.

All of the bandits had been captured, and so Hermes, Teddy, Justin, Wendy, April, and Grace regrouped together.

"Are you okay, April?" Hermes asked with concern as he looked at her bleeding leg.

"I've had worse," she lied. She had a limp, and so Grace had to support her. Justin muttered something about feeling his pain.

Hermes turned around, using his mental compass to determine where they needed to set course. "We must continue," he sighed. "The Dark Moon is approaching."

And so, without another word, the ragtag heroes set off into the distance to find the crystal that would determine their futures.

Thirteen

The Rogers Brothers

Thunder rumbled in the distance as gray clouds spread across the sky, so dark that they almost looked like smoke. A storm was coming.

With a cloak even darker than the clouds, Marco Victor Odious stood watching the sky. However, he was not watching the storm brew.

He stood in the front yard of a tall, blue house, although the house itself was not the most peculiar part of the yard for alongside it stood a monstrous willow tree with leaves as pale and green as blades of the most gorgeous grass ever viewed. It was Teddy's house.

A deep hole had been dug beside it. It had taken the bandits an extremely long time to make it so deep and dark, but it was necessary for his plan to work. Because of the recent precipitation, it was full of mud and grime. The willow tree's roots, old and gnarled but yet as beautiful as the tree itself, had been cut off

139

to dig it, and the roots now reached into the pit as if they were exploring the freshly created and yet purely disgusting hole.

However, the hole was not empty, oh no, for whispering could be heard from it. Inside it were multiple captives, including Teddy's own parents, his two uncles and aunts, and many of the villagers who had returned from their vacations. They had given up calling for help; they were tired, weak and hungry, for Marco Victor Odious was not generous in throwing down food for them. In fact, they were lucky to still be alive. They were surprised that such a despicable and evil man had not slaughtered them all as soon as they had returned unsuspectingly to their homes; instead, he had spared their lives, even though he had imprisoned them. He kept them alive, although not particularly well. The villagers had to come to the conclusion that perhaps he was not the horrible man that everyone thought him to be; still horrible, but not quite as murderous as everyone assumed. All except Teddy's parents, of course, who were constantly jabbering about how their capture would make breaking news; so much, in fact, that their fellow captors had to gag them at times to listen to see if Marco Victor Odious was plotting aloud or just to be at peace for once.

The odious man paid no attention to them, even as they started whispering about what could possibly be going on. He continued staring into the sky, listening intently for some sort of sign...

The thunder rumbled across the sky once more, but with it came another sound as well... the sound of a helicopter. Marco Victor Odious squinted and sighed. "Those fools," he muttered to himself.

The villagers whispered to one another once more. What in the world was going on?

High above the ground, the helicopter the villainous man had heard swayed in the high winds. However, the winds were not the only cause of the swaying, for the two pilots had never flown a helicopter until then.

As they lowered in altitude, crazed laughter could be heard from the ground, as if the two reckless pilots were enjoying the chaos as they prepared to land.

Marco Victor Odious's cloak flapped in the breeze as they finally prepared to touch down. However, he realized that they were about to touch down on his head, so he frantically ran away and jumped behind the willow tree! The townsfolk were worried that the flying contraption would land in their deep and dark prison, and so they hid themselves amongst the tree roots protruding from the dirt.

Luckily for the captives, the airborne device did not land in the hole they were imprisoned in, but unluckily for the pilots, it crashed onto the ground and fell onto its side.

The blades stopped immediately and the whole thing began to smoke uncontrollably. The helicopter door opened, and two coughing men jumped out of it.

The townsfolk backed up against the wall so they could see them better, and they saw that they were extremely eccentric-looking men.

The first wore a dark green coat covered in mold. He couldn't have been under six and a half feet tall, and so his scruffy partially-bald head reached up towards the sky. He had a long and tangled gray beard, which reached down almost to his waist.

The second wore a moldy coat similar to the first's, but his was deep purple instead. Unlike the first, he couldn't have been over five feet tall (and was rather plumper as well), although he too had a scruffy partially-bald head. Like the first, he also had a long and tangled beard, although because of his height it reached way down and nearly touched the ground.

Despite the severe height difference, the two men had to be brothers. Both looked about the same age (around sixty-five) and they both had round faces.

After their coughing ceased, both began chuckling hard. Marco Victor Odious glared at the pair of them.

"Vincent and Ulysses Rogers," he began. "I see you received my call?"

"All the way from Texas, Marco," Ulysses (the shorter one) said in an extremely strong southern accent; he sounded a bit like a cowboy because of it.

"Are you still committing those idiotic crimes that you were committing when I met you?" Marco Victor Odious sneered.

"'Course not," Vincent (the taller one) said defensively in an equally strong accent.

Back in the pit, Mrs. Evans looked at her husband excitedly. "It's Vincent and Ulysses Rogers!" she exclaimed. "The famous criminals from the south! This is the story of the century! Write that down immediately!"

"Of course!" Mr. Evans (who obviously did not have a pen nor paper to write it down) responded.

Vincent Rogers continued. "We work for Damien Komodo now, Marco."

Marco Victor Odious narrowed his eyes. "So… are you… immortal now?" His voice was tense and his eyes were full of absolute hatred.

Vincent and Ulysses Rogers, who did not notice these signs and would not have cared if they did, nodded and smiled. "Yeah!" Ulysses responded triumphantly, grinning evilly. "That's why we're so nimble and quick-like now! Unlike you, ya old lump o' soil!"

The brothers burst out laughing, and Marco Victor Odious looked like he was going to burst from anger. For one, he was much younger than them and so they had no right to call him "old", and he also despised being called a lump of soil. Secondly, if Damien Komodo had not betrayed him, he too would have been blessed with the gift of the Emerald of Eternal Life. In fact, he may have had full control of the emerald instead of his dastardly apprentice.

But Marco Victor Odious knew that he needed Vincent and Ulysses to complete his plan, and so he took a deep breath in and changed the conversation topic.

"So," he said, his eyes still narrowed, "where did you get the helicopter?"

"Stole it from the government or somethin'," Vincent said absentmindedly. "I don't really know, we just found it, snuck past the guards protectin' it, and hijacked the thing! What more do ya need?"

"And obviously you've never flown one before?" Marco Victor Odious said suspiciously, staring at the crashed vehicle with his eyebrows raised.

"Well, yeah," Ulysses said, confused about why his prior mentor was so focused on their flight.

Marco Victor Odious sighed. "Have you forgotten all of your training?" he yelled. "I taught you for years and now you're just carelessly hijacking helicopters?"

Vincent and Ulysses growled and then shared a malicious grin. "We're tougher than ya now, Marco," Ulysses snarled, although still smiling. "We don't care 'bout your rules anymore. So, what's the job you need done, anyway? Don't ya have those filthy bandits to work for ya?"

"Of course I do," Marco Victor Odious snarled back. "But even though I have the Thunder Crystal, those idiots are still gaining on me, and I fear they will reach me before the next Dark Moon. Your task is to go and stop them before..."

"You have that crystal?" Vincent asked. "Ya know, that one that contains them witches?"

"Show us," Ulysses said forcefully. His hands reached towards his belt, where weapons were presumably kept.

"Fine," Marco Victor Odious said, rolling his eyes. He pulled out the Thunder Crystal from his cloak. Its magenta glow cast light along the yard which was darkened by the clouds. The brothers' eyes shone brightly, but not only because of the crystal's light. Marco Victor Odious (who was a great deal smarter than the two of them combined) saw this glint in their eyes and quickly stowed the magical artifact in his cloak before they could act. Vincent and Ulysses frowned.

"Your task is simple," Marco Victor Odious said. "Find those who oppose me and defeat them, preferably as quickly as possible. Then, bring them back here."

"All right then," Vincent said, cracking his knuckles. "But we have one more question for ya."

"What more could you possibly need to ask?" Marco Victor Odious asked annoyedly.

"What's in that hole?" Ulysses growled.

Marco Victor Odious glanced into the hole. Everyone inside slowly backed against the wall and shrunk down to their smallest selves possible. The man who captured them smiled ruthlessly. "Those who have opposed me," he said softly. "And that is what will happen to you if you oppose me as well."

However, instead of having a frightening effect as he had intended, Vincent and Ulysses Rogers burst out laughing once more.

"Ya keep your slaves in pits?" Vincent yelled, chortling his head off.

"What's next, keepin' the sorcerers on potato farms after ya capture all of 'em?" Ulysses asked, guffawing as hard as Vincent.

Marco Victor Odious growled, wondering if Ulysses had asked the question knowing that whatever his answer was would be an opportunity to ridicule him.

"Just leave me," he growled fiercely.

"All right, pit keeper!" Vincent yelled and the two maniacs burst out laughing once more. Then, they sprinted into Metronome Woodland much faster than any seventy-five year old has ever ran.

Marco Victor Odious scowled bitterly just as rain began to fall from above.

As the first flash of lightning lit up the sky, the townsfolk worried if they would ever be freed, and wondered what in the world Ulysses Rogers had meant by "sorcerers".

However, one of the captives was not a villager. One of them had nearly no connection to them at all. And somehow, this captive was the most worried, for she knew what would become of the world if Vincent and Ulysses were not stopped. And so, she immediately began working on a way to escape, for she knew that she may be their only hope.

Fourteen

Hunter Havoc

The first drops of rain echoed throughout the forest. Lightning flashed threateningly just before a thunderous boom shook the leaves.

The sorcerer and his comrades were hours away from the little Alaskan village where Marco Victor Odious stood. They were practically close enough to see the small, blurry looking village if they were so inclined to climb a tree and peer into the distance. However, they did not, of course, because they wished to reach there as soon as possible. Unfortunately for them, they knew not of the roadblock that lay in their path ahead...

Hermes led the way with Teddy following close behind. April, who, after a few minutes of walking while being supported by her second-aunt, refused to be dependent upon another and used her spear as a walking stick. Wendy, determined but fearful, walked alongside April to make sure she would not hurt herself even more (although she need not have done so).

Grace walked behind them, clutching her spear like it was a parasol, and hiding right behind her was a more or less freaked out Justin who held his weapon like a lifeline.

Watt and Fade patrolled each side of the group in order to protect them from flanking. Teddy had no idea why Hermes had positioned his pets in this way; when asked, Hermes merely stated that an ambush was likely.

Teddy attempted to wrap his head around what could possibly hurt them now that the bandits had been defeated. Marco Victor Odious had to stay in his own village to keep the Thunder Crystal safe and (when it was time) release the Oracle. Perhaps one of Odious's devious trainees, Teddy asked himself. Or even a supernatural force like the witches... he could not decide which was more terrifying; after all, he knew of the witches' unique powers, per Hermes's discussion, but he knew not of how powerful those abilities were.

Teddy was afraid, but not as much as before. The ragtag adventurers had defeated the bandits, and Teddy was full of pride and confidence at this victory. He felt that maybe... just maybe... he would be able to get to Marco Victor Odious before the Dark Moon and stop him from unleashing the Oracle. However, sadly, he was soon to be proven wrong.

The wind whipped through the trees and blew the clouds so fast that they appeared to be swimming through the sky. The rain increased too in synchronization and blasted at them like cats and dogs being chucked off of the clouds.

Watt prepared to make an electric umbrella, but Hermes motioned him to stop. "We must save our energy for the war to come," he whispered. Unfortunately for him, Teddy overheard.

"War?" the confused boy asked.

Hermes sighed. "Yes, war is likely. The bandits delayed us, and... I sense something ahead."

"Marco Victor Odious?" Wendy suggested.

"Death?" a timid Justin squeaked.

Hermes shook his head and looked quizzically at Justin. Whether or not Teddy's cousin knew, the poor boy had changed much since the Spring Break where he had been taken from his home, Hermes thought. Wendy too was a different person. It was devastating to Hermes to think that their new gifts would be destroyed if the Oracle was released... but there may be nothing he could do. He had to fight as hard as he could, for the Sorcerer Council and his new friends. He had to vanquish the Oracle even if it meant destroying himself. He had to save the whole world. It was a burden he knew he was required to bear. It was finally his time to prove his loyalty to the Sorcerer Council.

"So... what waits ahead of us?" Grace asked after an awkward pause.

Hermes did not answer at first. Finally, he said, "Danger."

Teddy looked ahead of his master, wondering whether he was referring to the fact that the Oracle could soon be freed or some other force ahead.

If there was no rain, they may have had a chance to defend themselves. Unfortunately, because of the rain slamming down on them like a jackhammer operated by an angered narwhal, none of them were prepared for the attack to come...

An arrow sharpened to the point of killing whizzed through the air and hit a tree! While everyone whirled around to look, a dagger flew and nearly cut off Hermes's arm! Hermes gasped and turned in every which way to see where the attacks came from.

Two men jumped out of nowhere smiling devilishly as a crack of lightning lit up the sky and thunder roared ominously. The shorter of the two lunged at Hermes and put the dagger that he had not thrown right under the poor sorcerer's throat. The dwarf-like man knocked the wooden spear out of his hand so he was completely unarmed. The other hopped over to the shorter one's dagger and handed it back to him. Giggling evilly, he brandished his crossbow and pointed it at the others, particularly April and Teddy because they were closest to Hermes. Vincent and Ulysses Rogers had them trapped.

"So, Hermes Willowlands, that's ya name?" Vincent guffawed. "I never got the purpose of them stupid magical names."

"Pointless," Ulysses agreed. "Besides, it ain't legal bindin'!"

The men looked at each other and laughed hard. Teddy observed the two of them. Though they were hard to see in the combined darkness of the shadows of the trees and the rolling clouds, they appeared to be elderly brothers, and then it dawned on him that there were only two people who fit their appearances.

"You're the Rogers brothers!" Teddy gasped.

"Righty-o!" Vincent grinned.

Hermes gulped, the dagger still pressed to his throat. He was determined to stay steady. "You two are working for Marco Victor Odious?" he asked. "Is he not still mad at you for betraying him?"

"Ha!" Ulysses snarled. "He's too mad at Orion to be steamed with us."

"Orion?" Hermes asked suspiciously.

"Yeah, apparently Odious wanted some o' his brainwash potion or whatever for a slave he captured and Titus Orion brainwashed the guy to become his servant instead," Vincent said absentmindedly. "But why do ya care when you're gonna be dead soon?"

"Weren't ya listenin' to instructions?" Ulysses snarled at his brother. "We're to bring him back to Marco!"

"Right, right," Vincent said, rolling his eyes. "But if ya'll don't cooperate, we might just forget about our instructions."

"Of course," Ulysses smiled. "Now, all of ya, drop yer weapons."

Teddy gulped. He was anxious to lower his only defense. A quick glance at the others proved to him that they felt the same. Contrarily, Justin looked ready to stab them, thinking of them as ordinary old men.

"Now!" Vincent shouted, holding his crossbow higher. He turned it to Teddy, who was so petrified by the wicked device that he dropped his stick instantly. The others reluctantly did the same.

Making sure not to scrape the sorcerer's throat, Ulysses began to lead him into the forest.

Vincent pointed his crossbow at Grace (as she was the only adult remaining). He cocked his head towards his brother. "Move along," he growled.

Fearing to be speared by the villainous-looking tips of the arrows loaded into his weapon, Grace, April, Teddy, and his cousins obliged against their wills.

Teddy was filled with fear and dismay. This was it. They were captured. There was little to no chance of succeeding. They were weaponless, Hermes didn't have the Thunder Crystal, and Watt and Fade were nowhere to be seen...

Teddy whirled around! Watt and Fade had truly disappeared once again! He peeled his eyes, scanning through the rain, searching through the mud on the ground, looking for a sign of what might have happened to them. However, they had completely disappeared. On one hand, this was good; they were not captured and still could save them. On the other hand, they could have run away and abandoned them; there was no way of knowing because they were undoubtedly invisible, thanks to Fade.

Still, Teddy felt a spark of hope even through the combined despair of their capture and the pounding of the rain. Luckily, the Rogers brothers did not seem to notice that Watt and Fade had disappeared. In fact, Fade could have turned them invisible as soon as Vincent and Ulysses appeared so they would not even know of their existence.

Even if they did, they were too busy taunting Hermes to notice.

"Bet ya wanted to prove yer loyalty to the Sorcerer Council, didn't ya?" Ulysses laughed giddily. "Maybe ya wanted to be promoted to one of them Masters?"

Hermes did not respond and remained calm. Teddy made the assumption that he too knew of his pets' absence.

"Personally, I've never understood magic," Vincent chuckled. "All o' that mysticalness and whatnot... too confusin'. I think that any problem can be solved with a crossbow in my hand and a brutal attitude."

Ulysses agreed. "Yeah, when we met Damien Komodo and his second-in-command Oscar Windwick taught us 'bout that hocus-pocus, I thought it nonsense. My daggers ain't drawing energy from myself, so I say they're better."

Their reasoning reminded Teddy of Orion. Though he was still a sorcerer, Titus Orion had stated that he preferred his sword because it did not require his own energy. Teddy had regarded this as foolish, so it made sense that two idiotic murderous hunters agreed with this. Personally, Teddy thought of it as laziness and lack of inner strength. He then vowed that if he ever escaped from this now horrible adventure he would become a sorcerer and prove that even children have enough inner power and strength to use magic. If only he was in less danger he could do this and prove to everyone that your own energy can do anything… However, this seemed highly unlikely considering the situation.

Again he looked around for Watt and Fade, but they were nowhere to be seen. No paw tracks in the mud, no anything. He sighed in despair.

"Hey, whatcha snortin' 'bout?" Vincent grunted. Teddy jumped straight up in the air. Hermes quickly swiveled his head towards him in worry and got a jab from Ulysses's dagger.

"Answer me!" Vincent snarled. "You see any other sorcerers from the council? Whydya sigh?"

Teddy backed up in fear, almost tripping over April, who nearly lost her balance because she had been forced to drop her walking stick (which was a spear, of course). Justin gulped and

Wendy appeared to be trying and failing to think of a way to attack Vincent Rogers before he could do anything else. Grace just closed her eyes. Strangely, after regaining her balance, April looked to the sky, smiling slightly. Vincent stuck his crossbow right in Teddy's face and scowled at him, Vincent's finger pulling the trigger...

Vincent was forced backwards by an invisible force that seemed to fall from above! Mud splattered onto Ulysses, who instinctively turned towards his brother. While he was distracted, a cloud appeared under Hermes's feet and blasted him into the air like a hoverboard! Ulysses attempted to take a swipe at his flesh but being shorter than him he missed and also fell into the mud from the force of the attempted attack.

The cloud lowered next to Teddy and Hermes jumped off just as it disappeared with a puff. Hermes looked up, and everyone instinctively followed suit. In the sea of dark and normally misshapen clouds, there was one lighter one shaped like a beagle's head. Teddy almost laughed, surprised that he had forgotten that Watt, using his electrical powers, could turn himself into a cloud. Fade had also presumably been floating up in the heavens before crashing down on Vincent.

"That's why you were looking at the sky!" Teddy exclaimed to April.

"Well, if I had known you to be in serious danger, I would have done something, wouldn't I?" April laughed, eager to finally have a moment of peace.

A lightning bolt struck down on Vincent, who was beginning to get up. He yelped and jumped up in the air, only to find Watt sitting on him in beagle form! Watt bit the malicious hunter who fell to the ground once more.

Ulysses, who, like the majority of the population, was worse at throwing sharp objects while in a sitting position, accidentally chucked his dagger past Watt. It landed in the mud, its shiny blade being darkened by the combination of the dirt and the continuously thundering rain.

Fade jumped onto Ulysses and swatted his second dagger out of his hand. Hermes picked it up and collected the other as well. He then walked smartly over to Vincent (who was still being bitten by Watt) and reached towards his crossbow.

Unfortunately, unlike throwing sharp objects, shooting them from a sitting position really does not affect their accuracy, and if Hermes had not yelled out in fear for his pet, Fade would have been killed by the arrow shooting out of Vincent's crossbow and towards his own brother. She jumped into the air and bolted off of Ulysses, who stuck out his hand in front of him. The arrow struck his arm, and wincing terribly he plucked the sharp object off of him… revealing no blood.

Hermes gasped. "How could I forget!" he scolded himself, then spoke directly to the children in despair. "Vincent and Ulysses Rogers work for Damien Komodo! They're immortal! Run, children!"

Ulysses grinned, showing all of his unclean teeth. He ran (surprisingly fast for his waddle-like form) towards Watt and threw the sharp arrow like a dagger at the poor beagle. Watt turned into a cloud to avoid it and zipped towards the sky to gain leverage.

Ulysses then charged toward Hermes, aiming Vincent's arrow at his heart. Justin screamed. Wendy shrieked and pulled Teddy out of the way, and although he was pleased by this gesture he took off running into the trees. While Wendy cried after him and Justin commented on his stupidity, Teddy was nowhere to be seen in a matter of seconds. Grace hid behind a tree and put her head in her hands. However, Teddy's cousins seemed to forget about protecting April; she was left right in between the charging Ulysses and the rising Vincent. The latter pulled out his crossbow and cackled wickedly, aiming it at April. He pulled the trigger and the arrow whizzed towards her! However, she was prepared to duck, and as soon as the arrow was a foot away from her, she did so.

Vincent snarled and hurriedly lodged another arrow into his crossbow. April ran towards him as fast as her injured leg could carry her and prepared to grab his wicked device before he could shoot it once more.

Meanwhile, Hermes was backing away fearfully from the approaching Ulysses. However, Hermes was too slow for him; since Ulysses was immortal, there was no pain in his legs to slow him down. He lunged at Hermes and prepared to strike with Vincent's arrow in his hand! Fade hurried over to them and jumped on Ulysses. The hunter snarled (and if one had been listening closely they would notice that the hunters' snarls sounded exactly the same) and grabbed the poor cat by the tail! Fade started scratching him with her claws like those of velociraptors, but Ulysses aimed his arrow for her eye! He thankfully missed but gave her a scratch on the face that caused her to mew in pain.

Full of fury, Ulysses turned back to Hermes who had backed away just in time and had tears in his eyes from viewing his Bengal being attacked so brutally. However, Ulysses did not bother to attack Hermes again. With greed in his eyes (and still clutching the poor blue-eyed Bengal cat) he charged towards Justin and Wendy instead! Hermes gasped and ran over to assist them, wondering where in the world Teddy had gone.

Simultaneously, April was still fighting Vincent for his crossbow! She grabbed it, trying to yank it out of his spidery hands. Vincent yelled and hit her with the side of it, causing her to topple over. However, April was an exceptionally brave child and got right back up, kicking the tall man in the shins. He yelped in pain but stuck the crossbow in her face.

April, although valiant, intelligent, and fearless, was stuck in a position she could not get out of. Vincent grabbed her and laughed evilly. April prepared for the end.

However, two things saved her simultaneously. First was Teddy, who had been hiding in the trees waiting for a moment to attack, ran over to the bandit and tackled him to the ground! April, surprised but not caught off-guard, stole his quiver so he only had one arrow left: the one in his crossbow. Then, the second force struck. It was Watt, of course, who struck Vincent as a lightning bolt for the second time! He yelped once more, but being immortal, felt no pain. However, this time he was not as surprised and shocked as he was before, and quickly grabbed the beagle (who was sitting on the ground, recovering from the impact of his own attack) by the leg and cruelly used poor Watt to take a swipe at April's leg.

April was caught exactly at the wrong time and actually fell to the ground this time, her scarred leg now unusable.

Teddy, with tears in his eyes for his friend and the unfortunate fate that possibly awaited him if he did not move, got to his feet and retreated. He felt awful about leaving April, but he knew that Vincent was not targeting her and would not hurt her further.

Meanwhile, Ulysses also had the upper-hand. He finally had the sense to drop Fade (as Vincent had just done to Watt) but the pets were injured despite being closer to the Thunder Crystal than before; their powers did not heal and therefore had no effect on personal injury. The hunter had left Fade by a tree so she could not interfere and was taking violent, threatening swings at Wendy and Justin. They screamed and jumped away as Ulysses only laughed. Hermes was trying to knock him to the ground unsuccessfully while frantically crying out for Ulysses to take him instead of the innocent lives of Teddy's cousins.

Teddy was infuriated by Ulysses's laugh and stricken with fear for his cousins, but he knew that shouting out to them would not help. He quickly concocted a plan, unfortunately not seeing Vincent sneaking up on him from a few feet away.

Just as Ulysses had cornered his cousins and raised his daggers to take a massive swipe, Teddy ran up behind them and grabbed the handles! Ulysses gasped and then growled once he realized what was happening. Wendy laughed out in triumph and Justin just gaped. He stuttered as if to apologize for bullying Teddy earlier on but decided to tell him this at a different time.

Hermes ran over to assist, as Ulysses was attempting to elbow Teddy in the ribs. But, just as the weaponless sorcerer reached out to grab one of the daggers as well, Vincent's remaining arrow was shot and echoed throughout the stormy forest. It whizzed through the air and struck Hermes directly in the leg, and he fell to the ground teary-eyed and wincing in pain.

Teddy gasped and loosened his grip from shock. Ulysses smiled maliciously and regained control of his daggers. He turned around swiftly, shoved Teddy to the ground, and prepared to strike his dagger into his chest; Teddy was disposable and Marco Victor Odious did not need him.

He flung down his hand to kill the boy but Teddy rolled away swiftly. Unfortunately, Ulysses's other hand and dagger were free, and he used the dagger to make a jagged cut in Teddy's leg. He cried out in pain; his leg was as badly damaged as April's!

Teddy grabbed a tree trunk, pulled himself up, and ran as fast as his bad leg could carry him into the trees. Ulysses growled and held out his daggers in front of him as he looked through the darkness. He shoved Wendy and Justin to the ground so they could not help him and inevitably get hurt more from doing so.

"You ain't gonna hide forever, boy!" the despicable man yelled through the powerful noises of the thunder and rain. "You're the only one left!"

"Teddy, it's too dangerous and you're harmed as badly as I am!" April shouted to him desperately. "You have to give in!"

"When will you learn the right time to shut yer mouth?" Vincent snarled as he pried his quiver from her fingers.

Teddy breathed slowly fearing that speedy breathing would give him away. April was right on both accounts: he was both alone (besides Grace who was hiding in plain sight cowering in fear, although neither Vincent and Ulysses seemed to care about getting her) and he was as injured as everyone else. However, Teddy decided that he could still beat them if he had a strong enough plan. Besides, after watching his friends and family be pummeled by these malicious men, he would not go down without a fight.

Ulysses was jumping out from behind random trees attempting to scare Teddy. Vincent did the same after regaining control of his quiver. However, Teddy observed that they were fearful about actually finding him; when they jumped out from behind the other side of the trunks, they leaped back a bit when they saw something that looked like Teddy. He decided to use this to his advantage.

"You can't hide for the rest o' eternity!" Ulysses bellowed for the second time.

"The longer you hide, the more torture you get!" Vincent added nastily. By the sound of his voice Teddy could tell that he was extraordinarily close to him. He heard the slapping of his large feet in the mud. Teddy held his breath and readied himself for the attack...

Vincent jumped out from behind the tree and gasped. "Ulysses!" he cried out, but just before he did so he let down his guard for just a moment. Teddy tackled him to the ground and knocked the crossbow from his hands! Thinking quickly, he grabbed an arrow from the hunter's quiver. Even though he was immortal, the arrow could still be useful. He stabbed it through Vincent's moldy coat and into the tree, trapping the vile villain. Vincent grunted angrily, but he was trapped.

After seeing Teddy limp out from behind the tree safely, everyone cheered! Hermes laughed out loud despite his injury and April gave him a hopeful smile.

However, Teddy was not done. He peeled his eyes, looking for the second hunter, only to find that he had disappeared. Teddy immediately felt a stab of worry, ironically about being stabbed. But be that as it may, Ulysses was not waiting to attack Teddy; he was freeing his brother.

As Teddy wheeled around, hardly listening to Justin and Wendy converse about where they last saw him, Ulysses had cut the arrow from the tree, rescuing his brother. They stepped out with identical grins, and Teddy realized with regret that he had forgotten to take Vincent's crossbow and quiver.

"It's the end o' the road," Ulysses snarled. "Get up everyone. We have some walkin' to do."

Miserably, everyone got up. They were all injured in some way (Watt and Fade, the assets to their possible escape, were harmed the worst) and so there was nothing they could do. Ulysses imprisoned Hermes once more by putting his dagger over his throat. Wendy and Justin carried Watt and Fade, for even walking was difficult for the pets. Vincent pointed his crossbow at Teddy instead of everyone as he had done last time, as Teddy was now the largest threat besides Hermes.

Finally, as the rain hammered on, the miserable group left, right after April tugged Grace away from her hiding spot with extreme anger and annoyance towards her.

"That was really clever," she whispered to Teddy as soon as she returned to the hunters against her will. "I certainly didn't think of that."

"I didn't try hard enough," Teddy said miserably. "I failed."

"But you did try," April responded sympathetically.

For the first time since he had met her, Teddy disagreed with his wise and brave friend. However, that did not matter. The end of the world was now inevitable.

Fifteen

The Traitor

The pit was muddy, moist, and covered in grime, but the prisoners inside had much larger worries on their hands. Of course, they knew nothing of magic and very little of the fiendish plot that Marco Victor Odious and his despicable assistants had devised. However, they knew that something bad was to occur by Marco Victor Odious's sinister smile and the way he continuously looked eagerly over at Metronome Woodland.

In addition to this, the prisoners had not been fed that day, and this was presumably because their captor was so busy watching the forest that he did not bother throwing down even the tiniest portion of food stolen from one of the villagers' refrigerators. They had not eaten in days and their stomachs growled in pain.

Teddy's parents were worried sick. They assumed he had been kidnapped by Marco Victor Odious and possibly imprisoned in Metronome Woodland, and they also knew that the villainous man who had thrown them into the pitiful prison they were currently in had sent the two violent hunters into the woods as well. They were ashamed, too, for Teddy's cousins had gone with him, meaning that it was their fault that Wendy and Justin were lost in the Alaskan forest. Mr. and Mrs. Robinson and Mr. and Mrs. Monty (who of course had been thrown into the pit as well) comforted the two distressed parents and told them that it was not at all their fault. Unfortunately, there was nothing they could do to soothe their worry and suffering. Of course, Justin's and Wendy's parents were worried and stressed as well for their own children, but not nearly as much as Mr. and Mrs. Evans.

The other villagers were also worried sick but for different reasons, for one of the prisoners had actually decided to escape! She had dug a hole in the wall (this was easy due to the mud) and continued digging upwards. The villagers knew that if Marco Victor Odious found out that one of them was digging an escape tunnel, he would (at the least) torture them all until he found out where the escapee had fled to. The villagers had hissed for the crazy woman to stop her escape because she would be caught and all of them would be punished, but she insisted that she had to continue in order to stop a witch from being unleashed. The villagers had assumed her crazy; in their minds, magic was not real and Marco Victor Odious was merely robbing their poor village, not unleashing a monster.

Quite contrary to all of the townsfolk, up above Marco Victor Odious was undeniably happy. He grinned as he imagined the power he could have over the world if he really was able to unleash the Oracle… All he had to do was wait for the Dark Moon and those infernal hunters to return. He did not need his bandits any longer, for he had dozens of new bandits to serve him down in the pit just in case his plan did not work. Just before fleeing from the authorities (both normal police officers and Patrollers on the Sorcerer Council) he would force the strongest, fastest, and most mischievous townsfolk to join his side. That way he could attempt to steal the Thunder Crystal once more, and with so many bandits at his disposal, the sorcerers would not be able to stop him. Of course, before he did so, he would have to steal the Emerald of Eternal Life for himself... he was growing old and weary and if he wanted to punish Damien Komodo he would have to unleash the Oracle before he grew too elderly. In fact, Marco Victor Odious knew that once he did take control of the Oracle he would need to steal the Emerald of Eternal Life anyway if he wanted to live... However, he had decided that life did not matter any longer... only his revenge.

A distant crackling in the forest awoke him from his thoughts (the storm had died down slightly and so the sound could be heard). He smiled villainously as he watched the figures approach. The townsfolk backed up against the wall, attempting to see what Marco Victor Odious was so interested in. As the crackling noise grew closer, the villagers could see what it was more clearly, but that made things only more confusing for it simply looked like a small parade of silent, odd-looking people.

Ulysses led the way with his dagger still over Hermes's throat. Vincent was directly behind him with his crossbow pointed at Teddy (thankfully not yet recognized by his parents as they would have had heart attacks to see him in such a state). Following them were Wendy and Justin (also not recognized by their parents) who were still carrying Hermes's pets, and right beside them was April, whose leg was now so horribly injured that it was impossible to walk without being supported by someone. Behind them all were four people; one was Grace, and the other three were slightly taller and dressed in cloaks.

Vincent smirked once he saw Marco Victor Odious. "We got 'em for ya!" he said with a grin. "And we also picked up yer bandits... we were takin' so long to bring these guys back that yer dumb assistants caught up."

Ulysses gave one of them a jab with the back of his dagger.

"Hey, quit it, old man!" Dylan McCamel hissed.

"Yeah, we're on your side!" Michelle Laurens agreed.

"Ya disobeyed yer orders," Ulysses growled. "Yer as bad as yer fellow captives!"

Marco Victor Odious seemed to ignore this comment and instead took a long hard look at his recently incarcerated foes. He muttered to himself as he looked at them: Hermes Willowlands, of course, the three adolescents he knew were evacuated by Hermes, and a red-haired girl. His eyes stopped at her and he turned to Vincent and Ulysses.

"Who is this?" he asked forcefully, gesturing to April.

"Her name is Atch, sir!" said Vincent, saluting him mockingly.

Marco Victor Odious growled impatiently. "What about her last name? Atch who?"

"Gesundheit!" Ulysses yelled and the two brothers burst out laughing. Even Shannon Jones had the courage to snicker.

Marco Victor Odious was nothing short of outraged. "If you do not tell me who she is immediately, I will..."

"I shall speak for myself," April said bravely. Teddy gasped loudly, so loudly in fact that Vincent and Ulysses glanced at him and slowly pointed their weaponry in his direction. Justin and Wendy looked at her quizzically and undoubtedly worried. Hermes did not seem to notice; he was deep in thought, ostensibly thinking of an escape plan.

April continued rather forcefully. "I am April Finnegan, your second-niece. As the daughter of Seymour Finnegan, I demand to know what you did with him if you really didn't kill him... and why you turned from such a prestigious man to a despicable one."

Marco Victor Odious gaped at her. Both his tone and his eyes softened. "Is it truly you, April?" he asked.

She nodded in response and glared at him. "Now answer my question."

The bandits started as if preparing to run. Vincent and Ulysses stared at her. Ever since Marco Victor Odious had received his reputation as a master criminal and killer, no one had dared to speak so forcefully to him. April's second-uncle looked at her worriedly, but then narrowed his eyes.

"I did not try to hurt your father," he said. "I would never purposefully kill another member of my family... I never wished to hurt any of you."

"Yeah, right!" April said, almost laughing. Everyone, prisoners and captors alike, started as the bandits had done. The bandits glared at her, although Vincent and Ulysses looked frankly impressed. Marco Victor Odious looked at her with a strange expression... Was it sadness?

"Marco, this has gone on far too long," a new voice announced. "Dispose of the girl. It doesn't matter what she thinks when we unleash the Oracle."

The voice was drawling and cruel as if the person truly did not care about killing an innocent child. The tone was also arrogant as if the speaker thought themself smarter and more talented than all of the people listening combined. A woman stepped forward to Marco Victor Odious and turned to look at April. She was scowling, but her new expression did not completely obscure her face.

"Grace!" Teddy thought aloud, and he was not referring to the common practice of praying before or after a meal, for Grace Odious was the one who had such a drawling and despicable voice.

"But... I thought the traitor was Rowena!" Wendy squeaked.

"Don't be ridiculous," Marco Victor Odious said. "We fooled you. In fact, Rowena is down in that pit right now."

Teddy (who had wondered what the pit was for) looked down into its depths, as did Marco Victor Odious. The townsfolk shuffled around worriedly; they all knew each other as they were neighbors and so they correctly assumed that Rowena was the escaper. Fortunately for them, Marco Victor Odious did not look more closely. However, six of the villagers did not breathe easier. Teddy's and Wendy's parents listened closely with anticipation and fear, for they thought that they had heard their own children, and Justin's parents knew that their son had to be with them!

"Yes," Grace announced. "I am the traitor. I helped Marco Victor Odious escape from prison. I gave information to the bandits while they were spying on you in your sleep. I stole the Thunder Crystal."

"But... that doesn't make sense!" Teddy burst out. "Rowena was the one who ran away!"

"Explain yourself, Grace," said Hermes softly. He had trusted the villainous woman and cared about her only to find out that she had betrayed them all.

"I shall start from the beginning," Grace began in a regal voice. "I left a few things out of my sob-story. As a teenager, after I found out that Marco Victor Odious was a successful criminal, I was awestruck. I had no idea that villains could make such a profit. I was intrigued, thinking I could help my family by stealing and even killing. I was foolish, then. None of my family is worth helping. Besides Marco, of course."

Out of the corner of his eye, Teddy noticed that Marco Victor Odious's eye began to twitch. He looked at her with an expression that was clearly trying to hide severe anger. Nevertheless, she did not seem to notice. Teddy attempted to theorize why Marco Victor Odious was fuming at this comment, but his theories only made the situation more confusing.

"One day I finally found my brother. He trained me to be a criminal like he had trained many. He told me I was his best student; at first I believed that this was a brotherly sign, but I came to realize that he was genuine.

"I was with him when Damien Komodo and Oscar Windwick told him about the Emerald of Eternal Life. I was by his side as we journeyed to the cave. I saw how they betrayed him even though he was the one who figured out where the cave was and planned the entire expedition... assisted by myself, of course. They stole the emerald from his grasp and refused to give him the gift of immortality... even though he was the one who deserved it most, for he was their teacher and the one who taught them how to steal in the first place."

"How ironic," Ulysses snorted.

Grace did not laugh at his comment; in fact, she was scowling deeply, so intensely that Teddy could not tell whether she was scowling about Ulysses or Damien Komodo. He decided on a mix of the two.

"I was consumed by anger," Grace continued. "Despite being a hardened criminal, I loved my brother and it pained me to see him so defeated and wanting revenge. I hated the pain; I told myself that feelings were weaknesses to be avoided at all cost. Unfortunately, I could not get over my pain; I was stricken with sadness and there was only one thing I could do to get over it: help my brother get revenge.

"When Marco Victor Odious was training Damien Komodo, Oscar Windwick accompanied the teenager, for Windwick had seen power in Komodo and his gang and thought that the ways of sorcery could assist Komodo in his takeover. As I said before, Windwick taught him about the Sorcerer Council and magic and how much power Komodo could have if they took over the magical people. Windwick told him stories of the most powerful magical artifacts in the world: the Emerald of Eternal Life, of course; Orion's sword, which can poison anyone simply by the touch of its blade; the Scepter of Eight Flames, which was forged by a powerful sorcerer in the volcanoes of the Galapagos Islands; the *Magic of the Dark Moon* book, which is of course not magical itself but contains the knowledge of how to cast extremely deadly spells and curses; and finally, the Thunder Crystal."

Grace glanced at Hermes. "The Thunder Crystal is not as good a magical artifact as everyone thinks," she began, smiling viciously as she insulted the kind sorcerer she had already lied to and fooled. "Hermes Willowlands is not a special sorcerer just because he has it in his grasp. The Thunder Crystal is only special because of what it contains: the Oracle and her army of witches. Michael Nightwhale trapped them inside this crystal using the Interdiction Curse, and if someone got their hands on it they could bring the Oracle back on the Dark Moon.

"I reminded Marco of this tale, and he was interested," Grace continued, turning to Marco Victor Odious. "He could get his revenge against Damien Komodo and the rest of the world and I would finally be free of my sadness and all the weak emotions that flooded through me.

"Marco and his bandits set out to find the Thunder Crystal. We knew that it belonged to Hermes Willowlands, so they journeyed to the Enlightened Mountains. However, the authorities caught them while they were trying to take it from him, and my brother and his foolish associates were sent to the prison near Metronome Woodland. Marco Victor Odious managed to call me and told me of his unfortunate predicament. I obliged and used a series of bombs to blow down the prison walls, sneaking away just before the police could spot me."

"I shall take it from here, Grace," Marco Victor Odious told her. He had shaken off his glare but there still remained a cruel expression on his face. Again, it was unfathomable and Teddy could not tell if he was angry at Grace or just feeling villainous.

"My bandits and I dashed into Metronome Woodland," he began dramatically. "Those pitiful servants of mine built a base of sticks and stones so the authorities would not find us. They frequently reported back to me with information, as did Grace, and although I told my bandits about her I did not tell them her name for her safety's sake."

Teddy was growing more confused by the minute, not by the story but by Marco Victor Odious's strange comments. Could it be that he did not want to work with Grace or was something more occurring in his mind?

"The bandits informed me of the location of the Thunder Crystal and I informed Grace," Marco Victor Odious continued, studying the queer look that Teddy was giving him. "Her assignment was to go alone and find Hermes and the travelers, saying that she was lost in the woods. However, she found two others that helped her come up with an even better story.

"Her cousin and second-niece (which is you and your mother of course)"—he turned to April as he said this—"were hiking through Metronome Woodland searching for me. And, of course, you did not know that Grace was on my side and so she lied, telling you that she too was searching for me in order to save me from a life of crime. You and your mother stupidly believed her and Grace told you that she knew which direction to go in order to find me. Instead, she told you the direction to go in order to find Hermes Willowlands. This way, I had a spy on the inside."

April stared daggers at Grace. Her second-aunt had lied to her and made her part of the horrible plot against herself, her mother, and the people she now called friends. Grace smiled slyly, making April scowl even harder if such a feat was possible.

"Eventually, the three of you found Hermes Willowlands," Marco Victor Odious continued as he eyed his sister with another unfathomable look in his eyes. "Grace reported back to the bandits nightly while the rest of you were sleeping or else lost in your troubled thoughts. Then, every so often, the bandits would circle back to me to tell me the information that Grace had unveiled. This way I knew everything you were doing without being there. I knew what you were doing when you reached the Purple Mountains and encountered one of my many enemies, Titus Orion. I metaphorically journeyed alongside you as you escaped from Titus Orion only to run into a bear.

"Finally, that night, Grace reported to the bandits (who obviously reported the same information to me) that all of you were exhausted and the time to finally take the Thunder Crystal had come," said Marco Victor Odious, then turning to Justin and Wendy. "And, to make it even easier, you two completely broke down in the morning, yelling at each other, Teddy, April, and the others... that was when Grace realized that she could both steal Hermes's crystal and also lower morale by placing the blame on April's mother Rowena. Rowena was angry and acting intolerably, and so Grace knew that she could separate her from you foolish brats with ease, merely by telling you that she had to calm Rowena down; it was too easy.

"She grabbed the Thunder Crystal off of the staff while Hermes was looking at the fighting children and stuffed it in her pocket. She brought Rowena over to the forest where the bandits were hiding and told her cousin that she had been working for me all along. The bandits managed to restrain Rowena despite her vicious efforts, and Grace handed the Thunder Crystal to them, shooed them away, and began screaming that Rowena was gone and had stolen the Thunder Crystal."

Marco Victor Odious chuckled lightly to himself as if enjoying an amusing joke. They were staring back at him and Grace, wondering who was more despicable. Their plot was unimaginably clever and equally horrible. Each and every one of the captives (even Justin, who had considerably less heart than the others) were devastated by their unlawfulness and immorality. They wished they could have stopped Marco Victor Odious, Grace, Vincent, Ulysses, Dylan McCamel, Michelle Laurens, and Shannon Jones, but they all knew that it was far too late to do so.

"Now," Grace said, cackling gleefully, "all we have to do is wait for night to come, for the Dark Moon is finally here!"

Sixteen

The Oracle Speaks

Night swooped down on them all like a colony of bats for there was no moon to light up the darkness. The stars twinkled beautifully as they were the main attraction of the sky, but the captives hardly noticed them. They were far too worried about their own predicament.

Teddy had deja vu. He remembered when he had been held in that very yard by Watt and Fade, wondering if he would finally be able to experience the one thing he had waited for his whole life... magic. However, the situation had greatly changed despite the familiar place and position.

The bandits now restrained them, and although they were much less powerful than Vincent and Ulysses, the captives' hands and feet had been tied together, making it nearly impossible to attack the bandits. Wendy was nervously clutching her two cousins with her tied-up hands, whether wanting to protect them or wanting them to protect her, neither of them knew. Justin was quivering and muttering something odd about wanting to live on a peaceful dairy farm, and like with Wendy no one really knew what it meant or why it occurred.

Teddy was completely distressed despite Wendy's possibly affectionate gesture and Justin's entertaining rambling, and even a total stranger would be able to see why. The world would be destroyed (him along with it, of course) and he thought it would be his fault for failing to stop Marco Victor Odious. Obviously, it was not his fault; it was the Odious siblings' cruelty that would release the Oracle. Even if Hermes, Rowena, Wendy, Justin, April, and Teddy were to blame, Teddy was but a child and it would truly be Hermes's or Rowena's wrongdoing. And yet Teddy was such a compassionate and innocent young boy that he still felt that he was guilty of something horrible. It is truly one of the great tragedies of humanity that those who are guilty seldom feel so and those who are innocent often feel guilty about circumstances out of their control, and Teddy was experiencing this tragedy himself.

Meanwhile, the true guilty ones were feeling anything but dismayed, and so they too were experiencing this tragedy of humanity, although they'd hardly call it a tragedy. Vincent, Ulysses and Grace were sharing their plans of what they would do after the Oracle took over and giggling with malice at each others' ideas.

"Ima rule over the entire continent of Asia!" Vincent giggled. "It's the biggest, ya know, and tigers live there! I've always wanted to ride a tiger into battle!"

"Everyone knows that Asia's the biggest continent," grunted Ulysses as he rolled his eyes. "Here's a better idea: Ima rule over the Pacific Ocean! It's the biggest body of water and it's larger than Asia by far, and there are a bunch of sharks and other deadly animals that I would love to fight people with!"

"Those are the worst ideas I have ever heard!" Grace said rudely, although she was not wrong. "There will be no people to kill with your animals, idiots! The Oracle will want to kill everyone in the whole world besides the people who released her! Besides, do you really want to rule over such enormous places? Asia will be completely empty, Vincent, and you'll be alone in the middle of the ocean, Ulysses! Here is a much grander idea: I will force the witches to build me an enormous and luxurious castle to live in and the witches will serve as my slaves! Neither of you will be invited to stay there or even set foot in it, of course."

"That's a much lamer idea than mine, and I know that everyone will be dead except us!" Vincent growled annoyedly, clearly lying. "I was planning to ride my tiger into battle against... uh, ya know... other tigers?"

Grace sighed impatiently, not even bothering to respond.

Next to them, Marco Victor Odious was staring up at the sky, whether solemnly or eagerly no one could tell. The expression on his face could have been anticipation and annoyance, but it could have also been regret. He had been surprisingly distraught as soon as Grace had returned to his side... perhaps he felt threatened by his sister? Perhaps he wanted to be the sole commander of the Oracle and she was getting in the way? The only thing that everyone decided was certain was that Marco Victor Odious was lying when he said that he cared about his family. The captives had eventually given up guessing... quite frankly, they had given up doing anything. However, they were not the only ones who were watching him.

"Master Odious?" Dylan McCamel asked in a quivering voice. "Are you alright? Are you ill?"

"Of course I'm not ill," he replied gruffly, and looking down briefly he scowled at his henchman only to look straight back up at the sky once more. "Did I not tell you when I first hired you to steal the Thunder Crystal that unnecessary questions would lead to your disposal?"

Dylan McCamel quickly looked down in shame, but this threat felt different from the countless others. After exchanging a glance with Michelle Laurens and Shannon Jones, he knew that they too thought that the threat was lacking something... ferocity, definitely, but also meaning. It was as if Marco Victor Odious cared about nothing other than releasing the Oracle, although it was still unclear why he wished to do so. The bandits had talked it over countless times while trailing the path of the Thunder Crystal (such a tedious task had left lots of time for quiet discussion) and they had agreed that revenge against his enemies was not Marco Victor Odious's only reason for his strong desire to unleash the Oracle.

"Master Odious?" Shannon Jones asked carefully. "What would you like to do when we finally release that immense source of dark power? I mean, I'm just asking because the others were discussing it and I was kind of curious, you know..."

"You know well of my intentions," Marco Victor Odious said in a raspy tone of voice. "Unless you think that I'm hiding something from you?"

Shannon Jones thought this likely but despite being the most formidable and stubborn of the bandits, she was no match for Marco Victor Odious's wrath, and so she bowed her head in disappointment instead.

"He probably is hiding somethin' from ya," Ulysses chuckled. "Ya like yer secrets, don't ya Marco?"

"Sometimes I wonder what yer hidin' in that skull o' yers," Vincent put in, guffawing so hard that it sounded like he had a cold.

Marco Victor Odious did not respond. At first, it appeared that he was about to explode due to his reddening face, but it quickly disappeared. His eyes began gleaming with anticipation. He finally lowered his gaze from the sky and looked at the others.

"The sun has completely set," he said smiling. "It is time."

Vincent and Ulysses grinned viciously. Grace smirked and rubbed her hands together. The bandits started and held their captives even tighter than before. Marco Victor Odious himself stood up and withdrew the Thunder Crystal from his cloak. It no longer looked like a beautiful, magenta-colored source of light. Due to the circumstances, Teddy saw it as a pale, glistening weapon of destruction. He could barely breathe. The Oracle was to return and there was nothing he could do.

Marco Victor Odious fingered the crystal for a moment, then walked over to the willow tree where the staff lay. He lodged the Thunder Crystal into its place as his comrades watched impatiently. Finally, he reached into his cloak and withdrew a battered book for some strange reason. It was deep black (even though it was battered and faded) and it was extraordinarily thick (it must have taken Marco Victor Odious lots of strength to lug it around in his cloak).

"What's that book for?" Ulysses asked agitatedly.

"The Thunder Crystal is the door," Marco Victor Odious said softly, "and this is the key."

The Rogers brothers nodded, although not completely understanding the metaphor. To help them understand, Marco Victor Odious turned the book towards them, just out of Teddy's sight.

"What does it say?" he mouthed to April.

She looked back at him with a frightened look and gulped. "You're not going to like this," she whispered but nonetheless began to read the title. "*Magic of the Dark Moon.*"

Teddy could have been mistaken for a sheet of paper in the next moment due to how pale he turned. Marco Victor Odious turned the book away and flipped through the literary artifact of pure evil. He finally stopped at a page and his eyes gleamed with malice. A smile appeared on his bony face.

He gestured to Shannon Jones. "Hold this," he said in a quivering voice, but not because he was fearful. Shannon Jones walked over and held the book like she was a pedestal or a nursery school teacher showing young children the colorful pictures of a book. Marco Victor Odious then gestured to the other two bandits. "You two, bring the sorcerer over here," he said in an excited tone. "Vincent, Ulysses, guard the prisoners. I don't care what your opinion on the matter is, idiots, guard them!"

Dylan McCamel and Michelle Laurens pulled Hermes over to the book. Marco Victor Odious handed him the Thunder Crystal but withdrew a knife from his pocket. He positioned it right over Hermes's throat (as Ulysses had done earlier) so that he would not cast his own spell for his freedom.

"Cast the spell or die," Marco Victor Odious snarled in his ear. However, Hermes did not budge. His eyes darted worriedly toward his friends but he did not move a muscle. His villainous captor realized this. "I thought this might be the case... alright, cast the spell or that one dies."

He gestured now to Teddy, and Vincent walked over to him and aimed his crossbow at his head. Ulysses grabbed him so he could not move. Teddy was frantic. On one hand, he did not want to die, but on the other hand, he did not want to destroy the world. He weighed the two, and finally decided on the greater good. "Don't cast the spell!" he yelled in a quivery voice, but not the same quivery voice that Marco Victor Odious spoke in.

Hermes stared at Teddy with wide eyes. He then closed his eyes. Teddy wondered what his friend would do next...

He raised the Thunder Crystal and opened his eyes. "I am sorry, all of you," he sighed, "but I'm afraid I have no choice..."

Tears in his eyes, he stared at the pages of the *Magic of the Dark Moon* book. He raised his staff to the air and it began to crackle loudly! Suddenly, dark clouds formed in a circle around the Thunder Crystal up in the sky! Magenta-colored lightning shot down onto the Thunder Crystal and a cloud of darkness erupted from the magical artifact, obscuring everyone's vision. The captives waited in horror to see what would happen. They heard the cackling of Grace and the Rogers brothers. Finally, the smoke cleared, and they could see a large, jagged magenta line in the air... like a tear in the universe. The hole grew, revealing a dark abyss inside and thousands of glowing eyes of multiple colors staring at them. Finally, when the portal was wide enough, creatures began to fly out! Justin and Wendy screamed and April jumped into the air as if she had sat on a hornet's nest.

Teddy realized that Hermes's description of the witches had been the understatement of the century. Each witch was around five feet tall and floated a few inches off of the ground, making them look like ghosts, although they were far, far worse than ghosts. They wore cloaks as black as the night, but wore wasn't the right word… in fact, they appeared to be only cloaks, for no hands, arms, legs, or feet could be seen. The only living part of them that could be seen was their eyes: horrible, glowing, piercing eyes that appeared to just be colorful slits floating where their heads would be. They were awful, frightening, horrible, and ghastly creatures that should not even be seen in the most horrifying of movies.

Hermes's statement of what the different types of witches looked like was also a clear understatement. Yes, the Fire Witches had red amulets and matching eyes, the Earth Witches had green amulets and eyes of the same color, the Air Witches had amulets of yellow and matching eyes, and the Ice Witches had blue amulets and matching eyes, but Hermes had forgotten to mention the vileness of the colors. They were not bright or shimmery shades of those particular colors. Instead, they were disgusting, dark colors as if they were taken out of some sort of evil rainbow.

More and more witches continued to flood out of the portal. They formed a circle around the humans and animals and closed in as if imprisoning them. The villains laughed as they viewed the army they thought to be theirs, although unbeknownst to them, the witches were imprisoning them too. An uncountable amount of these despicable creatures now surrounded them, nearly obscuring the view of the willow tree and making the yard look like a convention of evil.

Finally, all of the ordinary witches had exited their place of confinement. Then, a slightly taller witch (around maybe eight feet tall) erupted out of the portal. He looked like his fellows (despite his height) but he had an orange amulet hung around his neck and blazing orange eyes. The witches parted and he walked through. The children shrunk back and the Rogers brothers pointed their weapons at the tall figure, fearing that he might attack them instead of their captors, not knowing who it was that set him free.

"The leader is coming!" he said in a rasping voice, although no one could tell if he was speaking to the witches or the humans. However, the tone of voice was not the eeriest part of cry for no one could tell where his mouth was. Teddy realized that this was the Elder Witch, commander of the Oracle's army. Unfortunately, he realized that this meant that the Oracle was to come out of the portal at any moment...

The portal brought on by the Interdiction Curse widened just a bit more and a mammoth of a creature leaped out of the magenta tear in the universe. The being rose to its full height, a horrifying twelve feet tall, and turned to the group of humans. She was a terrifying, vile-looking creature with glowing dark purple eyes and a matching amulet around her neck. But, most petrifying of all, she had giant, clawed hands made of glowing violet light as Hermes had described. She held them out in front of her as if prowling for a new victim.

"I have returned!" the Oracle bellowed in a horrible inhuman voice that echoed through the air like a gong of doom.

The bandits fainted, as did Justin. Grace shuddered as if overcome by a sudden feeling of coldness, and the Rogers brothers merely stared wide-eyed at the monstrous creature before them. Hermes stared at the ground in shame of what he had done, though he truly had been given no choice. April and Teddy looked as if they had been frozen while in mid-gasp. The only person who did not seem afraid was Marco Victor Odious.

He stepped up to the Oracle with barely a trace of fear. "I have demands for you!" stammered the despicable man. "I am the one who has released you and so I am your ruler! Now… kill all of these pitiful people except April and Grace!"

He gestured to them so that the Oracle would know who they were. Vincent and Ulysses growled at him, feeling extremely betrayed (although they were immortal). Grace stared at him quizzically. April returned from her petrified state and looked at Marco Victor Odious as if seeing him as her second uncle for the first time.

"After that, journey to find Damien Komodo to kill him!" Marco Victor Odious continued. "After that, destroy Orion's forces because of what he did to my…"

The man in black was interrupted by a booming laugh from the Oracle. "No one commands me!" she bellowed. "And there will be no survivors! Every single person in the entire world will die!"

She turned to her prisoners and reached towards them with her clawed hands. Grace stammered as if trying to find the right words. She had been wrong; the Oracle was not going to obey them. Marco Victor Odious turned pale. The Oracle wailed loudly as if she was a werewolf who was about to devour its enemies. "Destroy them all," the Elder Witch rasped, and the witches began to close in on the heroes and villains alike.

Everyone was so petrified that they did not even notice Rowena climb out of the escape tunnel she had dug and creep toward them with a dagger in hand.

Seventeen

The Final Fight

The Oracle raised her clawed hands and two purple beams of light erupted out of them. They hit Watt and Fade (who were still being held by Wendy and a semi-unconscious Justin) directly in their faces and they fell to the ground! Wendy gasped, and Justin would have too if he was awake. Watt and Fade, who had been injured by Vincent and Ulysses, surprisingly got up as if they had never been harmed. However, their eyes were dark purple, the color of the Oracle's amulet. They growled and snarled at Justin and Wendy, and then patrolled around the group, ensuring that no one could escape.

"The Oracle can corrupt animals!" Hermes gasped, suddenly remembering.

"Silence!" the Oracle commanded. "Prepare to die... after a session of torture."

Grace gulped loudly and stepped back only to step into a witch. The Rogers brothers winced in fear. Marco Victor

Odious looked like a man who had simply given up after finding such a large obstacle on the road to his victory. Hermes, however, did not look completely defeated. He looked nervous, but there was a tiny glimmer of hope in his eye.

The Oracle did not notice, as she had other things on her mind. "Attack them!" she yelled to Watt and Fade, and teeth bared, they both bent their knees into jumping positions, ready to strike at their victims...

Hermes raised his staff into the air and knocked Marco Victor Odious to the ground with the tip of the Thunder Crystal! He raised the staff even higher and then plummeted it down to the ground! The crystal emitted a powerful, blinding light, and a massive earthquake blasted through the ground making an enormous rumbling sound, and friend and foe alike fell to the muddy, sloshy grass. The witches, who of course floated above the ground, were still impacted and were blasted up and back from Hermes and landed a few feet away.

Teddy too had fallen to the ground, and he wondered why Hermes had used that particular spell if it disabled them too. Luckily, Hermes had seen something that he didn't, for of course Rowena was coming towards them! She was just out of the blast radius and so still on her feet! She now ran through the circle of dizzy witches rising to their, well, where their feet would be, and reached into her backpack and threw four daggers at the cousins.

"Catch!" she yelled quickly, forgetting that she had just thrown daggers at them. Teddy was the only one who caught his but it was only because of pure instinct. Justin's (who had fully awoken from his brief fainting spell) and Wendy's daggers fell by their sides and they picked them up quickly and pointed them at the bewitched animals, worried they would attack as soon as they got up. April was too busy expressing her gratitude for her mom's return to even notice her dagger as it fell to her side as Teddy's cousins' weapons had.

"Mother!" she cried out and ran over to hug her. Rowena embraced her daughter warmly.

"Rowena, how did you escape?" Hermes asked bewilderedly, his face like solid sunshine.

"Geez, how many daggers do you keep in there?" Justin asked, pointing to the backpack.

"We'll save the pleasantries and questions for later," Rowena said darkly, cutting short her embrace with her daughter. "We have to defeat these witches before they escape from the town!"

"If I can get rid of Watt and Fade's corruption, we may be able to hold them off long enough for me to report this to the Sorcerer Council!" Hermes said as he raised his staff to prepare to strike his corrupted pets who had fully risen to their feet.

"We'll protect you," Teddy said, attempting to sound braver than he felt. Justin and Wendy nodded their nervous approval, and April rose unsteadily to her feet (her leg was still in pain, as was Teddy's).

"You two are injured," Rowena noticed. "Teddy, April, you may protect Hermes and fight the witches, but make sure to stay safe. I'll help you if you need assistance." Teddy smiled at Rowena's kindness. She may have been tougher than her cousin Grace but that did not determine her morality.

Meanwhile, Grace herself noticed an opportunity to escape. "We have our chance!" she hissed to her brother. "This plan didn't work out, but who knows what we could do in the future!"

"We must take the girl with us," hissed Marco Victor Odious, gesturing to April. "She is a member of the Odious bloodline and will prove valuable to us!"

"When I first confronted you, you told me not to give in to weakness," Grace responded in retaliation. "Attempting to save our second niece could kill you… and me as well. We can always capture her later… she's with that sorcerer, she'll be fine." Grace smiled wickedly inside as she saw Marco Victor Odious's face fall. Grace of course did not wish to take April and did not believe that she would live, but she was a cruel person, much crueler than Marco Victor Odious, and did not care about any-one's life except her own. She was using her brother for his skills the entire time and only freed him and his comrades from jail so that she could benefit in the end. She was the one who had convinced him whilst in a time of pain and vulnerability to stoop to such an awful plan. And, unfortunately, sometimes the most dastardly and cunning people can corrupt their victims even after they have already corrupted them previously.

Marco Victor Odious looked at April preparing to fight the witches and hardened his resolve. "You're right," he said and gri-maced at the bandits waking from their fainting spells as Justin had moments before. "Get up, you idiotic lazy tadpoles! We're getting out of here!" The bandits quickly jumped up before they were stabbed by the dagger in Marco Victor Odious's hand and followed Grace through the mounting chaos. Marco Victor Odious followed behind them and shoved the Rogers brothers to the ground.

"Hey!" Ulysses shouted, waving his squat little arms in the air. "We're on yer side, ya know!"

"Don't bother with 'em," Vincent said, angrily getting to his feet. "We'll get outta here due to our immortalityness and return to good ol' Damien, but for now, let's take out as many beasts and people as we can!"

"Us versus everyone else!" Ulysses exclaimed. "I like yer thinkin'!"

They smiled maliciously and ran into the crowd of witches, Ulysses waving his dagger every which way and Vincent shooting and reloading his crossbow at an epic pace.

Meanwhile, the third group of humans was confused and nervous. This group was, of course, the captives in the pit. They could not see what was happening from inside the hole, but they could hear the horrific, bloodcurdling wails of the witches and could see the strange clouds swirling around in a circle like a hurricane. They had agreed not to follow through Rowena's tunnel because of the terrible noises, for they correctly suspected that Marco Victor Odious was up to more than looting their town. In fact, they suspected something that they thought was impossible up until then… magic!

Meanwhile, outside of the pit, the witches had adjusted themselves after the eruption from Hermes's staff and they began floating towards him. After all, they wished to wipe out the sorcerers before they got rid of the ordinary, non-magical population, and Hermes Willowlands was the only one with a magical artifact. And so, the legendary battle between the witches and the defenders began.

While Hermes fired spells at the corrupted Watt and Fade (who had both realized that he was up to something and were jumping around to avoid his shots), Rowena and the children circled him (always staying at most fifteen feet away so no person nor witch could slip through), deflecting the shots of the witches.

Armed with only a dagger, Teddy was forced to constantly leap to the side to avoid the shots from the monsters. He was targeted by a collection of malicious-looking Fire Witches. Their red eyes seemed to bore into him and their wailing sounded more like cackling as they approached him slowly. Teddy realized that Hermes had not lied when he said they could summon fireballs, for as they approached, flames appeared where the witches' hands would be, and when they grew to a certain size (about as big as his head), they would erupt from their hands and fly at poor Teddy at an incredible speed. He ducked this way and that until he remembered his dagger! It was not large, but just big enough to block a magically created flame flying through the air. As the next fireball blasted towards him he put his dagger out in front of him and held his breath. The fireball exploded in a sphere of flame and Teddy was left unharmed! As a bonus, his dagger was heated up to a faint orange glow giving it extra damage to any witches he was to destroy!

The Fire Witches wailed and advanced slightly more quickly. He blocked their flames with ease now, only occasionally feeling the actual heat of a blast. However, they were coming closer… and closer… and closer!

"Rowena!" he yelled nervously, nearly dropping his dagger as a large fireball zoomed at him. "How do you kill them?"

"I don't know!" she responded in a shout. "But I can't help you, I'm a bit busy at the moment!"

Busy she was indeed. As the most capable member of the circle of defense around Hermes, she was forcing many of the witches fighting the children to aim at her instead, knowing that she could save the poor kids by doing so. Unfortunately, she had taken on too many even for her to handle. Ice Witches sprayed tiny icicle chunks at her, attempting (and occasionally managing) to pierce her skin with the sharp shards. Earth Witches blasted thorny, disgusting, olive-green vines from the sleeves of their cloaks that seemed to be alive, as they wrapped themselves around her waist, trying to squeeze and suffocate her. Fire Witches, instead of throwing fireballs, blasted spurts of fire at her from their sleeves as if there were flamethrowers hidden in their cloaks. Air Witches materialized arrows made of cloud-like material and shot them at Rowena from above like archers, for Air Witches could of course float many, many feet off of the ground, unlike the other witches.

A glance to the other side of him showed Teddy that his cousins and April were also struggling. Wendy was battling a collection of Air Witches which were shooting large bubbles at her. When a bubble hit her it completely engulfed her and she was forced to grope around for a bit until she could pop it with her dagger. Even worse, every time a bubble that had im-prisoned her finally popped, her glasses fell to the ground from the impact of her hitting the ground and so she spent most of her time that could have been used for hitting the witches searching for her glasses. Justin was not technically battling any witches; a couple of Earth Witches were creating demon plants that rose from the ground under his feet and wrapped around his legs in an attempt to trap and immobilize him. Still, they were keeping a distance from him as he was aggressively whacking the plants with his dagger with a look of malice on his face. Teddy had never seen Justin that mad before, and he wondered if he was psyching them out or if he was just angry that his life couldn't be easier. Either way, it was weirding him out. April (who like Wendy and Teddy was fighting witches up close as she was not as terrifying as Justin) was battling a variety of types of witches. Only a few surrounded her, but because they were different kinds of witches it was difficult for her to focus on the incoming attacks. Although Rowena was fighting an even larger group of different types of witches, April had much less fighting experience than her mother (in fact, most people in the world had less fighting experience than Rowena) and so she was completely frazzled as she ducked to avoid fireballs only to get hit by barrages of icicles. All of them were busy, none of them able to answer Teddy's question about killing the creatures that they were battling.

A fireball that nearly burned his ear off brought him back into his battle. The Fire Witches were now in the reach of his dagger, the sleeves of their cloaks reaching toward him, for one of their powers was to inflame whatever they touched. He knew that if they touched him, he would be a goner, so with no guidance on how or even if the creatures died, he bravely stepped forward, closed his eyes, and swung his dagger at the nearest witch...

The witch wailed, but not because it was defeated. The dagger seemed to cut right through the monstrosity as if it were a ghost. Yes, its cloak was ripped in the place that the dagger cut through, and yet it still floated there, completely unharmed. Teddy gulped and backed away toward Hermes. He held out his dagger in front of him and gasped; since it had touched the cloak of the witch, it had turned a brilliant shade of fiery orange-white. Touching it now could severely injure him. He was glad that Rowena owned such high-quality daggers, as he could barely feel the heat despite holding on to the handle tight.

Another Fire Witch reached for Teddy's head, and he only blocked its cloak with his dagger just in time. He forced its sleeve away, but his dagger was now white hot and his hand now sweating deeply despite the quality of the dagger! The Fire Witches' fireballs flew this way and that, and other attacks came at him from behind them. He was losing badly, wondering how on earth they would win…

Then, Teddy focused on the dark red amulets hanging around their cloaked necks for the first time. He realized that the amulets must control their powers because of how the colors matched up with their elements and abilities. Then, he realized that if he could take away their evil powers, the despicable beings would die! And so, he reached his dagger forward and stabbed the closest Fire Witch right in the amulet. The creature wailed the awful wail, finally as a signal of defeat rather than anger, and it exploded in a cloud of darkness, leaving not a trace of amulet nor cloak.

Excitedly, he turned around to his struggling friends. "The source of their power is their amulets!" he exclaimed. "Stab the amulets and they'll explode!"

Rowena turned around to face him in surprise that the young boy had figured it out. Then, in the blink of an eye, she whirled around to face the witches she was battling and stabbed one of the Ice Witches in its blue amulet. It exploded in darkness as the Fire Witch that Teddy had annihilated had. Rowena smiled in glee and went to stab the amulets of the other witches surrounding her. Wendy and April did the same, although Justin was still whacking at the vines at his feet with no witches near him.

The Elder Witch gasped. "They have figured out how to destroy us!" he rasped to the Oracle. "Witches, be cautious, but remember, they are still lesser than us! Stick together and overwhelm them!"

Vincent and Ulysses had heard Teddy's discovery and now looked at each other with giddiness.

"Shall we take out some beasties, Vincent?" Ulysses asked his brother.

"Aye, Ulysses!" Vincent responded with a cackle.

A large crowd of witches were surrounding them, but they shoved through the crowd viciously until they were in the middle of the mix once more. Ulysses stabbed witches in their amulets to make a path through which the two could run without colliding into witches while Vincent shot down distant witches from afar and also the flying Air Witches with his crossbow.

Concurrently, Hermes was still fighting his corrupted purple-eyed pets. Lightning flashed at him from Watt's paws but with a swift motion of his staff a magenta-colored semi-transparent shield appeared in front of him and when the lightning bolt hit the shield it dissolved into nothingness. Fade (who not only had sharp claws but was also an incredible jumper) was attempting to launch herself up and grab the crystal off of Hermes's staff invisibly. Luckily, Hermes had some tricks up his sleeve and used his crystal to spray the air with a silvery mist, therefore able to see Fade's outline and blast her to the ground.

Alas, Hermes had not been able to hit either of his pets with a single Stopper Curse, which would reverse the curse that the Oracle had placed upon the beagle and Bengal. It was a curse that took much energy to cast and so disabled his movements for a few seconds just before he cast it, so his corrupted pets had plenty of time to leap out of the way. He realized he had to be a bit clever, and so he concocted a plan.

As Fade once more tried to knock the Thunder Crystal away with her claws, Hermes cast a Freezing Spell and a blue projectile-beam erupted out of the Thunder Crystal, hitting Fade! She was not frozen in the same way the Ice Witches froze their victims, for Fade did not fall to the ground; she was suspended in midair, completely unable to move. Watt shot streams of lightning at his corrupted friend, trying to free her in order to defeat Hermes, but his efforts were pointless because the Freezing Spell was a strong one and gave the sorcerer just enough time to cast the Stopper Curse and aim it at the immobilized Bengal cat...

A gray-green bolt of light erupted out of Hermes's crystal and hit Fade directly in the heart! The Stopper Curse not only turned her eyes from dark purple to their normal, bright blue shade, but it also canceled out the Freezing Spell and the cat fell to the ground. She mewed softly and went still; since the period of her corruption had ceased, so had her protection from pain, and so she now felt the scrapes and gashes that the Rogers brothers had given her earlier that day... more like yesterday, as midnight was finally upon them.

"I'm sorry, Fade, I'll cast a Healing Spell later," Hermes said softly to his cat and then spoke louder to inform the others of the development. "I have reversed Fade's corruption! As soon as I free Watt of his curse I'll heal you all and message the Sorcerer Council!"

"Well, hurry up!" Rowena yelled somewhat rudely, although this was not her fault. "I'm swamped and surrounded by witches!"

Although Teddy had told her how to defeat them, there were more witches than ever shooting projectiles of their element and using their other despicable abilities. The Earth Witches had almost completely covered Rowena with their thorny vines which left the Fire, Ice, and Air Witches free to bombard her with fireballs, ice beams, and cloud-arrows without her moving. She only defended herself by swinging her dagger wildly, luckily stopping the projectiles and keeping the witches away from her. Still, it was clear she would not last much longer on her own.

"Let me help you!" Hermes said quickly; freeing Watt from his corruption could wait if his friend was in danger. Unfortunately, Watt took this as a wonderful opportunity to strike Hermes with a bolt of strong lightning. The sorcerer fell to the ground and winced. "Never mind... Justin, Wendy! Help Rowena!"

Teddy's cousins ran over to the overwhelmed warrior, which unfortunately meant that he and April had to fight twice as many witches. They were more skilled than Justin and Wendy, of course, but they were also more injured. As the troupe of Ice

Witches advanced towards them, the two were having difficulty keeping up with the battle.

"On your left!" Teddy yelled to his friend who ducked just in time; an Ice Witch was about to blast her head off with a powerful ice ray.

"Thanks!" April yelled back and struck the witch with her dagger, only to have a large icicle created by another Ice Witch whiz by her head.

Then, the Ice Witches gathered in a group and raised their non-existent hands into the air. Flowing gray clouds appeared suddenly in the sky, and a powerful snowstorm began. The Ice Witches pointed at Teddy and April, and the snowstorm seemed to direct itself toward them. A chilly wind whipped at them like the gusts of the Purple Mountains. Snow blew into their faces and blinded them, sticking to their hair and clothes. The witches advanced once more, this time with the winning advantage.

Even worse, a collection of Air Witches in the sky zoomed over to them and started creating and shooting their cloud-arrows at the poor children. They could not be hit with their daggers as they were far too high in the air, and so the two just had to let them shoot and jump out of the paths of the arrows.

Rowena was still in trouble, despite Wendy's and Justin's best efforts, and the witches just kept coming. They hadn't even fought the Oracle yet, who was merely just watching them as she assumed that she would prevail soon. They were her entertainment, just a group of weaklings that would die on her command. Teddy was close to giving up. April fell to the ground as the witches surrounded her, courtesy of her leg. Teddy too was in pain, but he could not stop. He had fought for so long and so hard that he could not give up despite the overwhelming feeling of pain…

A magenta blast of light emanated from the Thunder Crystal! It passed through his body as if the blast did not exist, but oh, how it did exist. Teddy felt warmth flooding through his body, the snow in his hair disappearing. He felt joyful, hopeful, and exuberant, all of his pain disappearing instantaneously. The gash in his leg had disappeared and his clothes (which were muddy and disgusting, as he had worn them for multiple months and in that time frame trekked through a dangerous mountain range) felt as if they had just come out of the dryer.

He looked over at April, and she appeared to be experiencing the same sensation. She jumped up and stretched her hurt leg only to find that it was as good as new. She grinned at Teddy and they both looked behind at the man who had cast the spell.

Hermes Willowlands stood tall and majestically, his short hair and cloak billowing in the high winds. Watt and Fade stood on either side of him, both now uncorrupted and completely healed. Watt's body was crackling with electricity and Fade flashed on and off, her claws out and ready to strike. For the first time since Teddy had ever seen the sorcerer, the bags under his eyes were gone. He was awake, fresh, and ready to fight the hardest he had ever fought in his entire life.

"Everyone, keep fighting!" yelled Hermes. "I must message the Council immediately!"

Luckily, the healing blast that erupted from the Thunder Crystal did not work on witches for they were creatures of darkness that could not be healed. They were instead blasted back, as were the snowstorm and the vines that had tried to squeeze Rowena to death.

The witches wailed in anger and floated slowly toward them. Projectiles came, but Hermes had not uncorrupted the pets for nothing! Watt blasted his lightning at the icicle barrages and arrows, cracking the ice in midair and causing the cloud-like material of the arrows to explode in a poof. Fade slashed through the vines as they crept up everyone's legs, using her speed to jump from person to person. She also used her claws to slice through and pop the flying bubbles of the Air Witches. The only things they could not beat were the fireballs, but the daggers could, and so Teddy, April, Rowena, Wendy, and Justin repaid the favor by stopping the fireballs in midair as the cat and dog charged out of the way.

But then, the Elder Witch wailed and turned to the Oracle. "The animals they have uncorrupted have proved to be a valuable asset to them!" he howled in despair. "What do we do, my leader?"

"I must advance!" boomed the Oracle. "My powers are far greater than our feeble soldiers!"

The Oracle roared and made her way towards them, her clawed hands reaching through the air like she was grasping onto one of their throats. Teddy realized that she must have legs and feet too unlike the rest of the witches, for he now saw that she did not float above the ground and instead walked with footsteps that sounded like gongs ringing out. The booms echoed through the ground. Vincent and Ulysses stopped fighting and turned to the source of the noise. Marco Victor Odious, Grace, and the bandits (who had been sneaking through the mass of witches trying not to get killed) did the same. Watt and Fade stopped fighting as well and shuddered nervously. Even the witches ceased their attacks and turned to face their great leader.

"Hermes?" Rowena barked at the sorcerer.

"In a minute!" he yelled to her, staring intently at the television-like screen in front of him.

The Oracle increased her pace, and the booming came more and more often, becoming louder and louder as she advanced!

"Hermes!" Teddy yelled as he heard Justin whimpering and Wendy hyperventilating.

This time, the sorcerer turned to them with glee. "They're coming."

The Oracle stopped walking and booming as she had heard Hermes. Her eyes darted this way and that. And then, everything seemed to turn into pure light!

Eighteen

The Return of Orion

Nothing could be seen. The light seemed to flood through Teddy's eyes and into his brain, searing it with brightness and obscuring all of his senses.

If Teddy or the others had been able to hear or see, they would have heard the Oracle's pained wailing and a thunderous sound like a thousand giant bells ringing out in synchronization, and they would have seen the foggy outlines of eleven people of many different shapes and sizes slowly rising to their feet as if they had just fallen from the sky.

Then, the blinding light seemed to slowly seep out of Teddy's head and flow back into its place of origin (the center of the group of newly arrived people) as if a reverse explosion was occurring. Looking around wildly, he could see that the others had experienced the same sensation. The witches' eyes were closed as if they could not endure something so bright and powerful.

"Hermes Willowlands," a man with a low, powerful voice boomed. He approached them slowly, and Teddy could see that he was tall, slim, and dressed in a black robe.

"Is that you, Lord Knotweigh?" Hermes asked, still confused by the blinding sensation.

The man walked towards him and gently smiled. It was indeed Gregor Knotweigh, his defining bushy gray eyebrows, matching beard, and rectangular glasses showing them all that help had truly come.

The other figures behind Lord Knotweigh became less foggy as Teddy's vision adjusted and he could now see that they were the other members of the Sorcerer Council! Daffodil Coolwater, Hermes's blue-robed friend, smiled at the children and waved to Hermes. Rubus Woolsberry walked alongside her and the other Patrollers, huffing and puffing due to his diminutive stature and round belly. Ruby Hailheart strutted towards them, glaring at Hermes and barely able to control herself. Hex Turtlerod held his African helmeted tortoise with anticipation, smirking as he looked at the witches. Gina and Mercury Knotweigh stood by their brother's side, although Mercury appeared to be doing it against her will. The other sorcerers surrounded Lord Knotweigh as well, glancing around at the witches and Hermes.

"Every council member who is not currently on a mission is here to fight," Gina Knotweigh said proudly.

"But... this must be the most sorcerers united on a single mission in the history of the Sorcerer Council!" Hermes said surprisedly.

"The Oracle alive and prepared to attack is probably the most threatening power that has faced the sorcerers in the history of the O.W.S.C.R.I.M.," Lord Knotweigh reminded him. Then he turned to the other newly arrived sorcerers. "Now, all of you, protect each other, destroy the witches, take out the Elder Witch, but wait until every last witch has been annihilated to take on the Oracle! She is the strongest of them all, and until then all spells cast towards her will be defensive spells and shields!"

"Yes, Lord Knotweigh," the sorcerers said, bowing. Hermes bowed as well, as did Watt and Fade.

"You can defeat the witches by destroying their amulets," Rowena added. The other sorcerers were a bit confused as to why a non-sorcerer like herself had any idea what was going on, but Gregor and Gina Knotweigh nodded along.

By then, the witches had also overcome the glowing sensation. They wailed in anger and the Oracle held out her clawed hands in front of her, her eyes flickering on and off as if she was glaring so hard that her eyes closed.

"Hold on, Lord Knotweigh," Hermes said to his superior. "Before we attack, we must get these children out of here. They..."

"We're not going to sit back while you fight to your deaths!" Teddy interrupted, despite being somewhat frightened of Lord Knotweigh's powerful position. Justin, Wendy, and April were surprised by this outburst, but they realized that they agreed strongly.

"I'm not going to let my new friends and my mother die in battle," April said strongly.

"Yeah, what will you do, anyway, if you don't let us fight? Throw us into the pit of prisoners?" Justin asked loudly.

"You can just perform one of those Healing Spells if we do end up in danger!" Wendy persisted.

Hermes sighed, but Lord Knotweigh looked at them interestedly. "Hermes Willowlands, you said in your message that they helped fight the witches to protect you?" he asked. Hermes nodded. Lord Knotweigh smiled. "Then why don't we let them fight now? If anything, they have a lesser chance of death because they would be moving around."

Hermes pondered this. "I suppose you are right, Lord Knotweigh," he realized, smiling gently. "But we must give them weapons that are more powerful than these daggers if they want to truly be protected."

"Of course," Lord Knotweigh said. "Luckily, I am, not to be boastful of course, a bit of an expert on the matter."

He pointed his wand (it appeared to be made of long, sharp stone) to the sky and a humming noise erupted from its tip. The tip glowed a light gray, increasing in brightness every second. When it seemed that it could not get any brighter, Lord Knotweigh redirected his wand to the ground, and four blasts shot out of the tip. When they hit the ground, four longswords made of pure stone appeared in the slushy ground.

Justin gleefully picked up a sword and swung it around, his childhood dreams coming true. The others picked up theirs carefully, Wendy even holding hers as far away from her body as she could.

"I believe all things are in order, then," Lord Knotweigh said, his voice returning to the powerful and commanding tone that Teddy had heard him speak in when Hermes had called the Sorcerer Council the first time. He turned to the other sorcerers and pointed a bony finger toward the witches who were once again advancing toward them. "Attack!"

Justin charged into battle along with the other sorcerers and Rowena, slicing his sword through the air recklessly. Teddy and April followed him reluctantly and Wendy ran right behind them, trying not to be hit by any speeding magical projectiles.

Teddy tried to focus on defeating the witches, but he was more interested in the fighting methods and special abilities of the sorcerers. Hermes blasted magenta fireworks from his wand, the same ones he used when fighting Orion, and occasionally Watt or Fade would jump into a witch who drew too close to their master. If he saw a large crowd of witches packed together, he would shoot one of his Tree Spells into the ground near them and a fighting willow tree would grow in that spot, as he had also done with Orion.

Daffodil Coolwater used her wand made of green water plants (known officially as the Lily Wand) to blast water bombs at the witches, which, once exploded, blasted them to the side and stunned them briefly. After they had been stunned, Daffodil would create a whip made of seemingly pure water that was attached to the tip of her wand, and then she would strike the witches right in their amulets with the whip.

Rubus Woolsberry shot green bolts out of his lime green Plant Crystal. When they hit the ground, bright green flowering vines grew out of the ground, similar to the Earth Witches' vines but more colorful and generally happier-looking. The plants poked and prodded at the witches and tore off their amulets. Rubus also shot the green bolts at the witches themselves, and in that case, the vines would wrap around them like pythons.

Ruby Hailheart used her unique Shapeshifting Crystal to turn into different animals to defeat the witches. She morphed into an eagle when Air Witches were barraging the Sorcerer Council members and she used her talons to tear at their amulets. When Ice Witches started snowstorms, she turned into a polar bear (which would feel normal in such cold temperatures) and clawed at their amulets. When the Fire Witches would shoot their burning fireballs, she would turn into a monstrous rhinoceros and use her horn to ram through and destroy the balls of fire. Finally, she morphed into a tiger when the Earth Witches shot vines at her so she would be able to bite through the tough plants and lunge at the witches.

Gina Knotweigh was probably the strongest fighter of them all. Her messy golden hair whipped around as she swung her birch Plentiful Wand through the air. Yellow beams of light burst from the tip of the wand like lasers and cut through lines of witches at a time. However, she was not just using her wand for destruction, for the Plentiful Wand was specifically designed for casting strong Healing Spells (each wand and crystal has different strengths and weaknesses, of course). When she saw her allies in need of healing, a golden blast of light erupted from her wand and instantly healed everyone in the area.

Teddy was even drawn to look at the sorcerers he did not completely recognize. The French woman (named Juliette Matagot) used a crystal as black as night on a staff as weathered as the oldest tree stump in existence to shoot Deterioration Curses at the witches, making their cloaks crumple and their amulets shatter. The Chinese woman (named Kai-Ming Sharphelm) used her yellow crystal in the shape of a dodecahedron to summon spikes from the ground to pierce through the witches' amulets. A man by the name of Satyr Artemis shot silvery orbs at the witches using a wand made of sycamore. The most interesting by far to watch was the Scottish man (named Hex Turtlerod) Teddy had seen during the Sorcerer Council meeting. This was because he wielded neither wand nor crystal but instead a familiar, in this case, an African helmeted tortoise. He would throw the reptile into crowds of witches and it would explode, destroying all of the witches in the cluster. Then, the tortoise would teleport back into Hex's hands completely unharmed as if it had never exploded in a fiery inferno.

Teddy was still watching the many sorcerers when a massive purple bolt of darkness flew at him from ahead. He realized just in time and jumped out of the way and onto the ground. He heard a wail of anger and realized that the blast had come from the Oracle. He knew he had to keep moving if he was to avoid the attacks to come, so he lifted his sword high into the air and joined a group of sorcerers (including Hermes and Daffodil) at the frontlines of battle.

Teddy quickly realized from the number of witches he was fighting that the children and the sorcerers were clearly winning. The witches slowly backed away instead of advancing, and Teddy was able to get up close and slash their amulets without getting seriously injured. Hermes conjured up shields for his fellow fighters, shields that could be shot through on one side but not the other. This enabled his comrades to fire at the witches without getting attacked back, and it allowed Teddy (as well as April, Rowena, and his cousins, although he did not know exactly where they were fighting) to get up close and stab his long, thin, rocky sword at the foul creatures.

As Teddy glanced around him, he noticed fewer and fewer witches. There had to be only about a thousand... no, only hundreds now. His heart leapt at this; was there a chance for them to win?

Watt and Fade skipped past him and into the squadrons of witches, blasting them with lightning and invisibly slicing their amulets to pieces. He caught a glimpse of Marco Victor Odious and Grace retreating, no longer accompanied by their precious bandits (who had gotten caught up in a battle of their own and were miserably losing). Vincent and Ulysses were both ecstatic and petrified at the same time: ecstatic about the lack of witches, but petrified by the fact that the sorcerers might catch them and throw them into prison for the rest of eternity since they could not die.

Spells blasted, objects exploded at random, and the Oracle wailed in pure anger as she flung bolts of darkness at her enemies. As he fought a retreating pack of Earth Witches, Teddy smiled in glee, looking forward to returning to his house, back to normal... and maybe even not so normal. A vision went through his head of living with Hermes in the Enlightened Mountains, becoming a Patroller on the Sorcerer Council, going on even more adventures like this...

A deafening blast echoed through the air! Some of the sorcerers instinctively dropped to the ground with their hands on their ears while some merely closed their eyes in pain. Even the witches stopped, as they had done when the Oracle had decided to jump into the fight. Except this time the Oracle's eyes were not greedy-looking. Instead, they appeared angry, and even though Teddy thought it was hard to tell the witches' emotions by their glowing, flickering eyes, he could still tell that the Oracle was not unleashing one of her forces.

"Everyone, step away, for my takeover has begun," a man said loudly from behind them. Everyone instinctively looked back toward the voice and saw a large group of sorcerers standing at the edge of Metronome Woodland. Their wands and crystals were in the air signifying that they were the ones who had cast the Noisemaker Spell. The crowd parted and a man with glowing white eyes walked through the sorcerers.

"Orion," Lord Knotweigh said harshly, glaring at the despicable man. "You are forbidden to come in contact with any sorcerers of the council."

"Well, I broke that rule a little while ago, and it seemed a shame to go to jail without breaking it a few more times," Titus Orion said mockingly, looking at Hermes.

"What do you want?" Lord Knotweigh asked stiffly. "If you've come to redeem yourself in battle, you're making a mistake."

"Silly Gregor," Titus Orion smirked. "Though you are winning your fight, there remains a good number of witches for me to command. It's simple, really. Send my sorcerers into battle, wreak havoc, kill the Oracle, take control of the Elder Witch... then I'll have command of the army and you will be weakened."

"Drop your wands," Gina Knotweigh said nervously, her magical artifact pointed at Orion. Suddenly, a blast of darkness (courtesy of the Oracle herself) flew directly into the back of her head! A ripple of darkness echoed through her and she fell to the ground, alive but severely injured.

"Attack!" Orion yelled to his followers and they obliged.

"Get them all!" cried the Elder Witch, per the Oracle's instructions.

The battle began again, but for the sorcerers, it was more chaos than battle. Orion's troops blasted random spells at them, and although the sorcerers of the Sorcerer Council had more power and skill, Orion had the element of surprise and more soldiers. In addition to this, none of Orion's sorcerers cared if their fellows died, unlike the Sorcerer Council members who spent much of their time protecting their fellow members. In fact, because of the brainwashing job Orion had done on his henchmen, they were practically as mindless as the witches.

Teddy ran around like his pants were on fire, dodging witch attacks and the enemy sorcerers' spells. As he ran through his neighbors' and his yards which had been turned into a giant battlefield, he was no longer focused on fighting. It was strange how an arrival of a group of around twenty and the injury of one of their own (even if that one was someone as incredible as Gina Knotweigh) could change near-victory to near-calamity. The sorcerers were no longer organized in an orderly manner. They instead ran through the battlegrounds trying to kill the enemy sorcerers and the witches while simultaneously trying not to die. Teddy saw the very same Hex Turtlerod, Rubus Woolsberry, Ruby Hailheart, and all the rest running for their lives, even though they had been fighting valiantly only moments before.

"Children, Rowena, come over here," Hermes yelled to the kids and Rowena. Teddy ran over to him, having to duck as one of Orion's potions was lobbed over his head. April, Wendy, and

Justin appeared out of nowhere, Rowena at their side providing protection, looking ashen-faced and sweaty.

"You called us?" Rowena asked, bleeding slightly.

"I merely wanted to make sure you were all okay," Hermes said worriedly. "The odds are not in our favor, so if we're going to win, we'll have to band together with the other sorcerers."

"Is that even possible now?" Wendy asked wearily. "How in the world are we supposed to get the attention of all of these rambunctious sorcerers when..."

Wendy was not able to finish her sentence for the eight of them (herself, Teddy, Hermes, April, Rowena, Justin, Watt, and Fade) were pulled into the center of the battlefield as if they were paperclips next to an electromagnet that had just been turned on. Teddy yelled as he was blasted into witches as he and the others approached a strange, glowing object in the middle of the madness. The other sorcerers of the Sorcerer Council also appeared to be flying towards it against their will, but strangely, Orion, his followers, and the witches were sent flying away from it. When the group reached the glowing light, they seemed to bounce off of it and land on the ground next to it. Teddy quickly rolled out of the way as more sorcerers flew towards the light and bounced off as he did. Finally, it seemed like every Sorcerer Council member had arrived, and the light beam seemed to rise a few inches before creating an impenetrable ghost-like dome around the sorcerers, Rowena and April, and the three cousins. Teddy looked at the beam, fearful that it was the Oracle trapping her enemies (themselves) in the dome where she could easily destroy them with her poison gas power. However, the light was magically extinguished, revealing Lord Knotweigh holding his wand high in the air.

"I suppose that would do it," Teddy responded to Wendy's question, standing up dizzily.

"I have summoned you all into this secluded zone because our side is losing," Lord Knotweigh said, gasping for breath, because he was exhausted from the long bloodbath of a fight. "We desperately need to change our attack method, and I am out of ideas and quite frankly, exhausted."

"In addition to that, Officer Gina Knotweigh is injured!" piped up Rubus Woolsberry. The sorcerers murmured their agreement to both of these statements. Despite this, no one seemed to know what course of action they must take.

"We must recharge our energy, rest, and get back out with a new strategy," Lord Knotweigh continued, "but I cannot hold this dome for long and I need ideas!"

No responses, no plans.

"Anyone?" Lord Knotweigh asked. He was a strong leader, but everyone could still hear the desperation in his voice. He looked around hopefully but only saw faces of defeat and exhaustion. Teddy looked to Hermes but he was staring at the ground in sorrow. Rowena was glaring at the sorcerers, probably because she thought they were weak. However, April was not looking around at the sorcerers or at the ground; in fact, she was looking at Teddy.

"Teddy," she said, and even though she had said it somewhat quietly, the interior of the dome was so quiet that everyone turned to the young boy.

"Well, have you any ideas, young man?" Lord Knotweigh asked quizzically; he knew the boy had fighting potential or he would not have given him a sword, but this was a whole other level.

Teddy stood stalk-still as the sorcerers stared at him. He wanted to shout, "Why would I have any ideas?" but the words could not seem to make it to his lips. When he continued his silence, April pressed on.

"When we were fighting Orion in his tunnels, you took leadership when no one else would!" she cried out. "You led us to a victory! And after that, the time with the bear in the cave? You told us all that we needed to get out, and again you saved our lives!"

A murmur went through the crowd of sorcerers. Teddy still said nothing.

"She's right, dear child," Hermes said, beginning to smile. "When I first met you, you were the only one of your cousins who believed that I had magical powers! You convinced them of it and so led to their trusting of me!"

"I still don't trust you completely!" Justin said quickly, taking a small step away from the sorcerer, but nobody noticed nor cared about him.

"You helped me keep my current mission when speaking to the Sorcerer Council when I had that meeting in the forest," Hermes continued, smiling evermore brightly. "You spoke up to the Sorcerer Council even though you were nervous and quite frankly had no idea whether or not you would be punished!"

"When we were fighting Vincent and Ulysses Rogers, even when the rest of us were defeated, you attempted to come up with a plan and continue to fight, all by yourself against two immortal beings!" Wendy spoke up.

"Well, I suppose it sounds better when you put it like that," Teddy mumbled, and Rowena murmured something about missing a lot of the adventure while kidnapped.

"Teddy, whether you know it or not, you're a natural-born leader!" April said. "And now, we need your ideas. If we want to save the world, if we want to vanquish the Oracle and Orion and all of the wicked people threatening our planet, we'll need your inspiration and creativity!"

"Hear, hear!" Hex Turtlerod yelled, caught up in the moment.

"But he's so young!" Ruby Hailheart shouted annoyedly.

"Ruby, you don't seem to have any ideas yourself," Lord Knotweigh said sharply. "And if all of this is true, this boy is as capable as the rest of us, perhaps even more. So I say let him be heard, and my word is final."

"So, what do you think?" Rowena asked Teddy curiously. "Give us your ideas!"

The sorcerers, after listening intently to April's inspirational speech, now looked at Teddy with all ears. Teddy was still unmoving and still somewhat white-faced, but he had heard what April had said and now realized that it was true. Maybe he wasn't just a young boy fighting in a battle that he could not win. Maybe he truly was a natural leader. And so, with everyone staring at him, he looked up at them all and shared his thoughts.

"Well, if we want to defeat so many different kinds of enemies, we'll need to split up into squads," Teddy began, feeling somewhat ludicrous as everyone stared at him. "Now, the witches seem to be the least of our concerns as we were beating them before those jerks showed up, so how about the Patrollers handle them? Orion and his followers are a bit more skilled, so the Masters will handle them. Finally, we'll need the two Officers and you, Lord Knotweigh, keeping track of Marco Victor Odious, Grace (that's his sister, by the way), their three assistants, and Vincent and Ulysses Rogers. Of course, Lord Knotweigh, you'll have to revive your sister first, but once you have completed that job you may proceed. Mercury Knotweigh will cover for you in the meantime."

The sorcerers stared at him, unsure whether they should sigh skeptically or applaud at the plan. Finally, Lord Knotweigh spoke up. "Well, it may not be the most elaborate plan, but it is organized and surely better than our previous one," he said to them all. "Now, organize into your sections!"

For a moment, nobody moved. Then, everyone rushed into the sections that Teddy had told them to split up into. Since a few sorcerers were missing from the council, only five of the eight Patrollers (Daffodil, Rubus, Hex Turtlerod, Juliette Matagot, and Hermes, of course) and three of the four Masters (Ruby, Kai-Ming Sharphelm, and Satyr Artemis) remained, but it was enough. However, one person was missing, and Teddy couldn't quite place who until he looked at Lord Knotweigh and the group of Officers. Gina Knotweigh was on the ground, of course, groaning slightly and attempting to move her limbs, but the second Officer was missing.

"Where's Mercury Knotweigh?" Teddy asked the leader of the Sorcerer Council.

He furrowed his brow. "She must have denied my summoning," he said thoughtfully. "She is a very powerful sorcerer and can cancel out that kind of thing… I suppose she is still fighting elsewhere or maybe searching for Marco Victor Odious. The latter would be better, but it would be better still if she was with us…"

"In that case," Gina Knotweigh said, slightly stuttering from the Oracle's blast of darkness, "I better join in the fight." She rose to her feet unsteadily and, raising her crystal, she cast a feeble Healing Spell for herself. Despite its weakness, it seemed to help her, and she stood up straight.

Lord Knotweigh looked at his youngest sister worriedly but then sighed. "I suppose we need all hands on deck… I will protect you as much as I can." Gina Knotweigh nodded in response.

"I have one more question about your plan, Teddy," Lord Knotweigh asked. "What shall you, Rowena, and your friends do while we battle?"

"I have something planned for us," Teddy responded. "We have a special agenda. While you all distract the witch army and our other enemies, we will take down the Elder Witch and the Oracle."

Lord Knotweigh began to object, saying that he was too young, but remembering that Teddy was the one who had been able to organize his underlings and who had come up with the plan himself, he finally agreed.

And so, the Lord of the Sorcerer Council raised his wand once more. "Ready?" he yelled to the council members turned fighters. When no one objected, he flicked his wand, the dome disappeared and everyone rushed into action.

Nobody who had not been inside of the dome seemed to notice it disappear, as they were too busy fighting. Orion's most recent order was for his servants to slay the Oracle and capture the Elder Witch, and so they attacked the witches with increased ferocity, pushing their way toward the two most powerful witches. But then, the Masters and Patrollers got into the fight, and now, organized together and with the element of surprise on their side instead of Orion's, they began to win.

Ruby Hailheart morphed into a giant elephant and ran through the clashing witches and members of the Orion cult, knocking them apart and separating them into two simpler groups: the witches and the servants of Orion. Then, she knocked the witches close to her away with her giant trunk and turned to Orion's army. With Kai-Ming Sharphelm and Satyr Artemis, the other Masters, she began fighting the confused sorcerers, throwing them up into the air with her trunk and kicking them into their fellows with her giant feet.

Meanwhile, the five Patrollers fought the witches with the same surprise-attack advantage as the Masters. Rubus used his Plant Crystal to trap the witches while Daffodil fired spells at them. Hex Turtlerod took care of the large crowds of witches with his exploding turtle. Juliette Matagot, who was incredibly gifted at distance spells in addition to her Deteriorating Curses, sniped the Air Witches and other otherwise unreachable witches with arrows made out of darkness created from her crystal. Hermes blasted them with firework spells as he had done before, while Watt used his clouds to bring him and Fade to Air Witches high up in the air or just a group of witches too far off for even Juliette Matagot's spells.

Lord Knotweigh and Gina Knotweigh were also benefiting from Teddy's grouping strategy. Vincent and Ulysses (who had been wreaking havoc on all three sides of the fight) had been caught off guard by Lord Knotweigh's sudden attack and the duos then dueled. Despite their unfair advantage of immortality, Vincent and Ulysses were losing the fight (though of course not dying) and Vincent was running out of arrows to shoot, leaving Ulysses as the primary attacker. Lord Knotweigh used his wand to create giant meteors, launch them into the sky, and drop them down on the devious brothers while his faithful sister used Stunning Spells to stop them and make them easier targets while also providing Healing Spells for the pair of them every once in a while. Eventually, when Vincent had run out of arrows and Ulysses's daggers had lost their sharpness from overuse, the two were forced to flee into Metronome Woodland. Lord Knotweigh began to follow, but Gina Knotweigh stopped him.

"They are out of the fight and prove to be no immediate threat," she said. "We can catch them later, but for now, we must focus on Marco Victor Odious."

"You're right," Lord Knotweigh said. "I suppose we just might be able to catch those horrible men later." And so without further ado, the two took off and the Rogers brothers ran cackling into the distance.

Meanwhile, the Masters and Patrollers were also succeeding greatly. After about an hour, only a couple hundred witches remained and Orion's forces were in shambles. Orion himself had gotten into the fight and threw his potions every which way. However, the three Masters had gotten smart about it and started using spells to explode the dangerous potions in mid-air (green poison, blue sleeping potions, red bomb potions, and purple hypnotizing potions, although he rarely used his purple potions in combat), therefore spilling them on Orion's comrades, and using Attraction Spells on the yellow healing potions to bring the good potions into their own hands and so enabling them to heal themselves instead of Orion's slaves.

However, although both Lord Knotweigh and Orion had joined the fight, one of the three leaders had not, and that was, of course, the Oracle, for not only were the sorcerers doing their job, but so were Teddy, April, Justin, Wendy, and Rowena. Although Justin had freaked out when Teddy had told him that their job was to fight the Oracle and the Elder Witch, when Teddy told him that the other option was to be thrown into the pit of prisoners, he had reluctantly obliged.

Luckily, Teddy had planned out the timing of the attack perfectly: right after the Patrollers had started mowing down the opposing witches, the Oracle turned her army and angrily started shooting bolts of darkness at them once she realized that the Sorcerer Council had managed to pull themselves together. The Elder Witch also turned to the witches and frantically bellowed orders at them like an enraged military general. While they were both distracted, Rowena and the children gripped their weapons hard and ran toward them, engaging in battle.

Justin and Wendy took on the Elder Witch, who was no real threat by himself but necessary to distract as he was the only one who could order the other witches around, while Rowena, April, and Teddy took on the much more powerful Oracle. Up close she did not use her bolts of darkness for as soon as she could form and shoot one, the enemy she would be trying to shoot would have already jumped out of the way, and, even worse for her, could get extremely close to her amulet. And, of course, there were no non-human creatures to corrupt, as Watt and Fade were off helping Hermes. Instead, she used her other two abilities: spreading poisonous gas through the air and levitating objects and people.

Whenever Teddy, April, or Rowena got too close, the Oracle held out her clawed hands and putrid, vile-colored gas rose from the ground and surrounded their heads like fog. The stuff stung like a thousand needles piercing into their flesh and their very skin felt like it was being obliterated from existence. In other words, as soon as the poison rose from the ground, the current attacker (be it any of the three) would have to fall back and jump into another position.

The Oracle's levitating powers were in some ways better and in some ways worse. They were better because, well, no one had to endure the biting sting of the poisonous gas. But on the other hand, if levitated high enough and dropped, the attacker in question would risk breaking a bone. The Oracle would grab fistfuls of air as if grabbing onto some invisible object and then would raise her hands high up into the air, forcing the nearest person up as well. The only possible way to avoid it was to get out of her range before she raised her hands, and so the three of them were sent scrambling away from her and the amulet around her neck that needed to be destroyed every time it appeared she would try to levitate one of them.

Regardless of these powers, every time Teddy, April, or Rowena attacked, they learned from their mistakes and tried again with improved tactics. The Oracle, on the other hand, grew angrier at every attempt they made and so became more vulnerable each time they tried. But in addition to being vulnerable, she also grew more powerful with every angry attack she targeted.

After a good many more minutes of battle, only about one hundred witches remained, but two of those one hundred were the Oracle and the Elder Witch who had still not been beaten. Eventually, the Oracle had gotten so full of anger that instead of targeting them individually, she unleashed a cloud of poison in a circle around her and the three brave fighters were sent running away.

"Enough of your attempts!" the Oracle wailed. "Your side may be able to defeat my soldiers, but you will never defeat me! I am too powerful and you are all alone! As you can see, your feeble friends are still fighting vigorously and running out of energy."

Teddy turned to look at them and saw that this was true. The witches were starting to overpower the Patrollers and Orion's forces were finally starting to weaken the Masters. A new plan was needed, a plan that he would have to play a valuable part in...

"Teddy, look out!" April yelled and frantically pulled him away from a bolt of darkness from the Oracle as she cackled wickedly.

He ducked down, but he wasn't paying attention to his near-death experience. In his head, he formulated a new plan, one that he didn't have time to explain but he might just be able to act upon...

"April, I'll have to borrow your sword," he said quickly, taking it from her before she could answer. "Rowena, destroy the Elder Witch when they're distracted."

"What do you mean?" Rowena asked. "What's going on?"

"Plan B," Teddy said, and without a moment to lose (because he couldn't afford the loss of a single second), he threw April's sword right at the Oracle's amulet! She wailed and ducked out of the way before it could pierce through the material from which it was made, but Teddy's plan had not been to kill, but instead, distract. The Elder Witch turned to the Oracle who turned to Teddy, who sprinted toward his own house before the Oracle could hit him with a bolt of darkness. Rowena watched him curiously but suddenly realized his intentions, and while the Elder Witch was staring at his leader who had almost died, Rowena threw her dagger at top speed right into the commander of the witches' amulet. The Elder Witch exploded in a cloud of darkness, and multiple things happened. To start with, Justin and Wendy (who had been previously fighting the Elder Witch) jumped because they had not seen the dagger coming. Secondly, the Oracle ceased her fire on Teddy and turned to the cloud of darkness where her assistant had once stood. Thirdly, after Orion noticed that the Elder Witch had been annihilated, he called for his forces to retreat into Metronome Woodland, for his plan could not function without the Elder Witch alive. Finally, and most importantly, every single witch besides the Oracle that was alive froze. The Patrollers took advantage of this and started slashing witches to the ground, Hermes even managing to take down ten at once with his booming fireworks. However, they were only briefly stunned, for they soon returned to fighting. But without a commander, they were not united as one and started attacking not only the Patrollers but also each other. It was an odd sight seeing creatures instantly turn on each other and fight for themselves instead of a greater power. Teddy wondered how Lord Jenna Everest had ever thought that these creatures could help save the magical people as he ran towards his blue house. However, he was glad that they were the way they were, because with the absence of the Elder Witch, every single witch (besides the Oracle) was exterminated within minutes.

With the witches and Orion's forces gone, every present member of the Sorcerer Council except for Lord Knotweigh and the Officers (who still had work to do) turned toward the Oracle. Rowena and April had realized Teddy's plan and started pressuring the Oracle toward the willow tree beside Teddy's home.

Meanwhile, Teddy tore through his house with more speed than he ever had before. He raced up the stairs and burst into his room. Everything was covered in dust from its lack of use and Justin and Wendy's air mattresses lay deflated on the ground, completely unmoved. His bed was made and he felt a small tear come to his eye thinking about how long he was away from his parents and how worried they must have been. Taking a second look, he saw that his bedroom, despite being covered in dust, was completely clean. His parents must have spent hours there, wondering where in the world he was.

However, there was no more time for recollections or tears. Teddy thrust open his window and jumped onto the branch of the willow without caring about the wobbles; he was so used to danger by then that he had become immune to worrying over trivial things such as this. He ran across the wide branch of the willow and through the natural tree-fort without bothering to glance at the beauty of the pale green leaves and the amazingness of it all. He scanned around for a branch that brought him lower to the ground; if he jumped from the current height, it would give him a broken leg. When he found one he took a deep breath, clutched his sword of stone carefully and jumped off of the branch he was on and carefully landed on the lower branch. Then, he saw her.

Rowena and April drove the Oracle closer and closer to the willow tree. Teddy smiled and prepared himself in a launching position. She was just out of range... just out of range...

Then, the mother and daughter pushed the beast directly under the willow tree, and Teddy held his breath and leaped down right in front of the Oracle! If she could make any human noises besides speaking, Teddy was certain that he would hear a gasp come from her cloak. He raised his sword, at the perfect distance and angle for a direct hit in her amulet... the sorcerers held their breath as they watched to see if Teddy's attempt would work or if he would die...

But something unusual happened in a split second. The Oracle seemed to shrink as if suddenly greatly aging and her eyes and amulet glowed white. Then, she spoke in a raspy whispering voice that only Teddy could hear. "When the Lord of the Sorcerer Council falls, a force even more powerful than the witches will wreak havoc upon us all... a dark force fueled by both the Dark Moon and the elements of life will soon gain more power than ever imagined..."

Teddy, his sword over his head in striking position, was confused and bewildered. And before the Oracle could say anything else, he struck her amulet with the very tip of his weapon and she exploded in the largest cloud of darkness of all.

Then there was silence.

Nineteen

The Prophecy Unveiled

Cheering erupted throughout the small village. Cries of huzzah shook the trees, and the great green weeping willow beside Teddy's house swayed majestically as if it too was celebrating their victory. Lord Knotweigh and his sister ran over to the sorcerers asking what all the commotion had been (as they had been attempting to catch the bandits and the Odious siblings), and once they saw the cloud of black dust where the Oracle had stood, they grinned like schoolchildren. Gina Knotweigh was so exuberant that she almost let go of the person that she was holding tightly.

"Lord Knotweigh, Officer Knotweigh, who is it that you've caught?" Hermes asked curiously. Gina Knotweigh and her brother shared a smile and she walked closer to them revealing that the person had medium-length curly blonde hair and black-rimmed circular glasses, and they knew the only person that it could be was Grace. She scowled and struggled against Gina Knotweigh's grip but she was far too weak to get away.

"We have not been able to get a single word out of her, but we have reason to believe that she and her brother decided to split up and fend for themselves rather than sticking together," Lord Knotweigh informed them.

"And did you catch the three bandits?" Teddy asked the siblings. "And what happened to Marco Victor Odious and the Rogers brothers?"

Gina Knotweigh opened her mouth but then closed it. Lord Knotweigh sighed. "Vincent and Ulysses Rogers escaped, but Marco Victor Odious's assistants were left behind trying to protect him and Grace," he said solemnly. "They died in an explosion brought on by the Fire Witches. We wouldn't have known since they were incinerated, but we happened to look over at them as the explosion occurred."

Everyone was silent for a moment. The bandits may have been vicious and evil, but they were just Marco Victor Odious's assistants, not murderers. In fact, as far as they knew, Marco Victor Odious could have forced them to be his servants.

"And... what about Marco Victor Odious?" Teddy asked quietly.

"Marco Victor Odious escaped," a new voice announced. Even though Teddy had only heard it once, it was so cold and vile that he knew that it had to be Mercury Knotweigh. And so it was, standing right behind them, having snuck up on them while they were cheering.

"Where have you been, Officer Mercury Knotweigh?" Lord Knotweigh asked his sister forcefully.

"Searching for him," she responded coldly, seemingly immune to Lord Knotweigh's forceful tone.

"And did you find him?" Gina Knotweigh asked her incredulously.

"I only had time to see his shadow and cloak whip by as he dashed into Metronome Woodland," her older sister responded absentmindedly.

"Why didn't you persist?" Gina Knotweigh asked sternly.

"What makes you think I didn't?" her sister spat back.

"Even though you technically followed Teddy's plan, you still refused to fight before his plan had come into action," Lord Knotweigh said scoldingly to the middle child of the Knotweigh family. "We will talk about your insubordination later back at Nightwhale Castle, Mercury."

"Fair enough," she said in the same cold voice from which Lord Knotweigh could sense no emotion. She strutted away to look at the Oracle's remains and Lord Knotweigh turned his focus to Teddy, who had walked over to ask him a question.

"Lord Knotweigh, should we let down a rope or something of the sort for the prisoners?" he asked.

"Not yet," the oldest Knotweigh sibling responded. "We must clear all signs of magic first. They must not know about any of this."

"One more thing…" Teddy began, but Lord Knotweigh had already gone to fetch a few of the Masters to help him clear the area of any signs of abnormality. Luckily, someone did notice Teddy and walked over to him.

"What were you about to say, Teddy?" Hermes asked him kindly.

Teddy hesitated as he wondered how to phrase what he was about to say to the sorcerer. "Well, before I destroyed the Oracle's amulet, she sort of shrank back and her eyes and amulet turned bright white," he began.

"Yes, I noticed something of the sort, despite my being farther away," Hermes responded slowly. "Go on."

"After that, she spoke in a raspy voice and said..." Teddy paused as he tried to remember exactly what it was that the Oracle had told him. Once he remembered, he recited it. "'When the Lord of the Sorcerer Council falls, a force even more powerful than the witches will wreak havoc upon us all... a dark force fueled by both the Dark Moon and the elements of life will soon gain more power than ever imagined...'"

Hermes was as still as a rock.

"Do you think it was a prophecy of some sort?" Teddy asked. "I mean, she is called 'the Oracle'."

Hermes was silent for a moment more, but then he finally spoke. "I hope that you are wrong but I think that you might be right," Hermes sighed. "Lord Jenna Everest did start rumors that the Oracle had the power to tell the future... that may have been why she was named so in the first place. But just because the Oracle said something does not mean that it is guaranteed to happen. It could have been a threat, although by the words she used that is unlikely. And even if it does turn out to be true, sometimes prophecies predicted by sorcerers or other magical beings are not a hundred percent accurate... and she never did directly state that the Lord of the Sorcerer Council was to die..."

Hermes's voice trailed off. "I'll tell Lord Knotweigh about it later," he decided, then smiled slightly. "In the meantime, why don't we focus on more positive things, like the fact that you just killed the Oracle! Our journey is over because of your bravery, creativity, and quick thinking!"

Teddy laughed and smiled in triumph, but his smile quickly fell off of his face. He decided to tell Hermes about his predicament despite the fact that Teddy doubted he would be able to help. "Actually, I'm a bit sad that our journey is over," he said. "Not that I wanted the Oracle to win of course... I just mean that I enjoyed being around sorcerers and using magic every once and a while... I guess what I really want is to just be around magic."

Hermes pondered this. Teddy looked into his eyes, hopeful for a hint of a smile or perhaps just a glimmer in the eye. However, Hermes was as unfathomable as Marco Victor Odious until he finally decided to speak. "On one hand, I stand by what I said earlier," he told him. "I will not be able to train you fully... yet. However, if she lets me, I plan on training one person this summer: Rowena. I have not told her yet, but she has questioned me about it before and I think it is time I train her. In fact, I was going to ask her about it now but then I saw a hint of curiosity in your eyes and decided to answer whatever question you might have had. Anyway, she and April (as April has but one parent and no other trustworthy family member remaining, she has to stick with Rowena) would journey up to the Enlightened Mountains come July and learn the ways of magic. Rowena is an adult and so can be trained freely, unlike you. But luckily for you, the Enlightened Mountains are not a long way away from here, and although I will not be able to fully train you, I might be able to sneak in a few lessons."

"Really?" Teddy asked surprisedly, as he had not expected convincing Hermes to be that easy. However, he quickly recovered from his state of shock in order to seal the deal. "All right, I think we have an agreement."

"Good!" Hermes Willowlands said with a nod and then walked over to Rowena who was surrounded by other sorcerers congratulating her on killing the Elder Witch and assisting in the defeat of the Oracle. Teddy watched for a moment as Hermes squirmed his way through the crowd to finally ask Rowena her opinion on the matter, but he was soon interrupted by a tap on his shoulder.

"Teddy?" Wendy asked as he turned around. Justin stood by her staring at the ground. "We would just like to say that... we're sorry."

Teddy stared at them. "You mean for the things that you did before we went on the journey or the way you behaved during the journey?"

Justin laughed a little but then became solemn again. "Both, I guess," he said, finally looking up at Teddy's eyes. "I guess I was... kind of a jerk."

"Me too," Wendy said loudly, a little more eager to speak than Justin. "I just wanted to make sure you were always safe, since, you know, you're the youngest cousin, but I guess I was kind of overprotective and obnoxious. Justin was just trying to be funny and impress you, but he was also a bit obnoxious."

Justin shot her a dirty look but then remembered that he was apologizing and responded with a simple "yeah".

"So... we're sorry for treating you foul over the years," Wendy said. "We really..."

"No, guys, I'm sorry," Teddy interrupted her.

Justin looked at him quizzically. "Why the heck would you have to be sorry?" he asked.

Teddy grinned. "Well, if you could read my mind, then you would know how gruesome some of my revenge plans against you guys were."

Wendy laughed and Justin yelled in mid-guffaw, "Now that's what I'm talking about!" Then, Wendy pulled them all into a suffocating group hug that the other two only got out of alive because of Teddy's swift reaction time which was quintupled after the long and perilous journey. Then his two cousins went over to apologize to Hermes for all the trouble and disruptions they had caused during his mission that was meant to actually save them, and Teddy's thoughts were once more interrupted, this time by April.

"So, I guess this will have to be goodbye, then," she said.

"We'll see each other again soon," Teddy assured her despite the sorrow he too felt.

"I suppose so," April agreed. "Who is to say when, where, or how, but I do think that we'll see each other again."

"That's a nice way to put it," Teddy responded. "You are much, much wiser than I will ever be."

"You have other, better traits," April insisted. "I meant every single word I said in the dome; it wasn't just to get you to give us a plan."

"Well, thanks," Teddy said, doubting that he really was all of those things that she had said. "So... I guess I'll see you soon."

"When both of us least expect it," April responded. Together, they walked over to Rowena, who was still chatting with Hermes.

"Good news, Teddy," Hermes told him. "Rowena has accepted my offer, and chances are that you'll be able to learn some magic this summer in addition to seeing the three of us again."

"The three of us?" April asked, looking from her mom to Hermes to Teddy. Then she laughed. "I guess we'll be seeing each other again quite sooner than expected!"

Teddy laughed as well, and the four of them happily spoke about the arrangements for their last few minutes together as the Masters and Gregor and Gina Knotweigh erased every trace of magic from the tiny Alaskan village. Finally, Lord Knotweigh approached the four of them and beckoned Justin and Wendy over to them.

"It is time for us to be going," he said, his eyes smiling at them from behind his glasses but his face remaining serious. "Hermes, you shall return to your mountain with your two pets and prepare lessons for your new apprentice... if she said yes, that is."

"I certainly did," Rowena said proudly, even though she wasn't really supposed to respond.

"Rowena, you and your daughter may make your way home through the woods," Lord Knotweigh said, turning to them. "However, do not show your faces around this area; the villagers must not notice anything or anyone suspicious... not that I am saying I suspect you, of course, but they might think you are the reason that these cousins disappeared."

Rowena and April nodded to show they understood. Lord Knotweigh finally turned to the cousins. "Now, Justin and

Wendy, I give you permission to tell your parents about your journey, but only your parents. Do you understand?"

The two nodded, but looked at Teddy oddly. He too was confused. "What about me, Lord Knotweigh?" the puzzled boy asked.

"Correct me if I am wrong, but I have reason to believe your parents are journalists?" Lord Knotweigh asked him with a hint of sternness in his voice. "If they hear that magic exists, do you think they will want to immediately inform the entire world?"

"I... I suppose so," Teddy said with a sigh. "But please, I'll make them promise not to tell anyone else, even their closest friends and family! I must tell someone about our journey! It is too much of a burden to bear!"

Lord Knotweigh raised a hand to silence him. "What makes you think that they will keep to their promise?" he asked. He was not being rude; by his tone of voice, Teddy could tell he was merely being curious. Luckily, this was a question Teddy found easy to respond to.

"Trust me, they'll be so distraught that I've been away for so long and happy that I have returned that they would promise me anything," the twelve-year-old said confidently. Lord Knotweigh examined him for a moment, peering at him with raised eyebrows, but finally lowered them and made his decision.

"That seems fair enough," he responded. "But if they don't keep their word, you and your family shall be in serious trouble."

"I'll force them to keep their promise if I have to," Teddy informed him, not willing to admit his desperation.

"All right then," Lord Knotweigh said. "Now that all things are in order and all signs of magic have been erased from the premises, it is time for you all to say your goodbyes."

The three cousins looked over to Hermes, Rowena, and April. Teddy didn't know about his cousins, but he did not want to see these people go. Not all of the experiences the six of them went through together were positive (actually, nearly none were), and yet he still felt affection for them simply because they had experienced a journey together that changed every single one of their lives. A bond like that was completely unbreakable, not by Marco Victor Odious, the Oracle, Titus Orion, or even the complete traitor Grace (who was not allowed to speak to anyone and was still held carefully by Gina Knotweigh). But unfortunately, all good things must come to an end, and so the six said farewell to each other.

"Farewell, my children, and my new apprentice," Hermes said sorrowfully, the bags under his eyes magnified because of his sadness.

"I'll never forget you guys," Wendy said to Hermes, April, and Rowena.

"You better let us come on your next adventure!" Justin said defiantly to Hermes.

"I'll miss the feeling of peril that we experienced together," Rowena said, and Teddy almost laughed until he realized that she wasn't being sarcastic and that she truly did love the thrill of danger.

"See you next summer, Hermes, Teddy, and maybe even Justin and Wendy if they happen to stop by!" April said in a glass-half-full way.

"This was probably the best experience of my life," Teddy admitted to them. "There is no possible way I could forget it, and I don't want to."

The six of them smiled sadly at each other when Rowena finally cut the tension. "Well, Lord Knotweigh said we ought to get going, so I think we should start heading back home," she told them.

"Where do you live, anyway?" Teddy asked April.

"Maine," she said. "We parked our car in that big town a few miles away from here on the outskirts of Metronome Woodland. It will be a bit of a hike and a bit of a drive, but it'll be nothing compared to our adventure."

The cousins' mouths dropped and Hermes stared at her incredulously.

"What?" she said jokingly, knowing that it was a ridiculously long distance.

"Nothing," Teddy said quickly. Rowena looked at them all as if only a coward would think that a drive from Maine to Alaska was a bit long.

"We have to go now," she said, tugging her daughter along. She waved her goodbyes to the others. However, Teddy still had one last thing to say to her.

"April!" he yelled, running to catch up with them. They finally stopped and she turned to him curiously. "I just wanted to say that if the bandits weren't lying and your dad is alive, then I hope you find him." Teddy wondered if what he said would calm her or only make her nervous, and for a second he worried that his final goodbye had gone the wrong way.

But April smiled hopefully at his words. "I hope so too," she responded. "Thanks for all you did to help me confront my uncle."

"No problem," he told her. "And even though I'll be extremely far away, I hope you know that I'm still supporting you, this time in finding your dad."

"Whoa, hold on a second," Rowena said quite seriously, an intense expression on her face. "My husband's alive?"

"I'll tell you about it later," April said with a grin. Teddy gave her a short smile, and she extended her hand in a jokingly business-like manner, which Teddy shook. Then, April and her mother walked away into Metronome Woodland as April began to tell her about how the bandits said her father was alive.

When Teddy turned back, Hermes was already standing on a rising cloud with his cat and dog, the cloud created by the latter.

"I shall see you soon, Teddy," Hermes yelled down to him. "But in the meantime, I must return to the Enlightened Mountains, by the order of Lord Knotweigh."

"I'll miss you, Hermes!" Teddy yelled back.

"Just one more spell before I leave!" Hermes shouted back. Teddy curiously looked up at the Thunder Crystal, which was gleaming in an even more brilliant shade of magenta than he had ever seen before. Then, a blast erupted from the crystal and hit the mammoth willow tree! Teddy gasped, but he needn't have, for the tree did not die or explode. Instead, its gnarled branches straightened out and its trunk turned a lighter shade. However, neither of these even came close to trumping the greatness of the new color of the leaves. They had turned a soft shade of pink that was so beautiful and eye-catching that he wondered if he would ever be able to look away. The leaves that were previously ripped or dead from lack of water repaired themselves, appearing healthy and gorgeous. The sight was indescribable, and although Teddy wanted to look at his three friends as they disappeared, he, unfortunately, found himself drawn to look at the tree.

When he was finally done marveling at the spectacle of magic and nature, he noticed that Lord Knotweigh had created a ladder made of stone with his wand. He nodded to Teddy, Justin, and Wendy, and said, "It is time." He walked over to the pit as Gina Knotweigh and Kai-Ming Sharphelm carried the ladder. He looked down into its depths, careful to show only his face so no one could tell he was wearing a sorcerer robe.

"Hello!" he called to the non-magical townspeople. "I am a police officer who was sent to capture Marco Victor Odious and all of the other people involved in your kidnapping!" Teddy cringed at his acting skills while Justin tried not to laugh. "We will throw down a ladder for you while we go and catch them!"

"Was there a battle out there or something?" a villager asked. "I heard some crazy noises!"

"There was a bit of a struggle, but it will be fine!" Lord Knotweigh responded.

"Are there three children out there?" a quivering voice wailed. Teddy thought it sounded extremely familiar, and so he snuck just a little bit closer to the hole to look inside, only to realize that it was his mother who had spoken.

"Yes, there are!" Lord Knotweigh responded. "They are fine! Do not worry, they will tell you everything. Now, if there are no further questions we shall lower down the ladder and leave!"

Luckily, his acting period was over, and he gestured to Gina Knotweigh and Kai-Ming Sharphelm to position the stone ladder. After doing so, Lord Knotweigh motioned to the Sorcerer Council and they gathered around his position.

"Goodbye, all of you," he told them, "and good luck. I consider it an honor to have met all of you."

And with that, they disappeared in a surge of light, just like how they had arrived, although this time Teddy had the sense to look away before they did so. Then, right after the remnants of the blast had cleared away, the six parents emerged from their prison and gasped at the sight of the kids (even though Lord Knotweigh had told them that they were present).

The parents ran toward their children, their faces full of happiness and joy. Wendy's parents hugged her like never before. Justin's barraged him with kisses. Teddy's mother and father did both.

"We were so worried about you!" Mrs. Evans said, speaking at the speed of light. "We just knew that you were kidnapped by Marco Victor Odious! That's what happened, right?"

"We're so sorry, we rushed out of the house so quickly that we forgot that our house is right next to Metronome Woodland, which is where he escaped from in the first place!" Mr. Evans exclaimed at a speed equal to his wife's, if not faster. "We thought we would never see you again, and then that monster of a man imprisoned us mockingly! Teddy, we are so, so, sorry..."

"I accept your apology!" Teddy said quickly before they could apologize even more. "And, actually, I wasn't kidnapped by Marco Victor Odious... not really, at least."

"Really?" Mrs. Evans asked. "Then what happened? Surely you didn't run away?"

"No, I didn't," Teddy said. "But before I tell you, you have to promise that you won't tell anyone anything about it."

"Oh, of course, darling!" his mom responded. "But what's so secret about it? And what is 'it'?"

Teddy laughed at how easy it was to convince his parents not to blab. "I'll tell you in a moment," he said, chuckling. "But first, let's help our neighbors get out of the pit…"

Twenty

The Sighting

A flickering fuchsia flash filled the small, dimly lit cave. Inside, Rowena held a bronze staff with a crystal seemingly made of iron atop. She hammered it on the ground in anger and April (who sat on the cold ground in a relaxed manner) laughed.

"Mother, abusing your crystal won't help you cast a Blinding Curse!" she chortled.

"Oh, really, like you could do any better?" her mother responded playfully. She handed the bronze staff to her and April gripped it with a look of mock smugness on her face. Then, she pointed it at Hermes (who was acting as the test subject for Rowena's spells and curses), and a bright fuchsia bolt of light blasted from the crystal and exploded right in the ragged sorcerer's left eye.

He winced in pain for a second, then performed a Healing Spell with the Thunder Crystal and a rejuvenating blast of magenta light flooded through their hearts, making them sigh with relief. "Well done, April!" Hermes cried. "I don't mean to be rude, Rowena, but it may be harder for you to become a sorcerer at your current age, as children and people who are… er… generally more full of energy are best at casting spells."

Rowena gave him the stink eye while April laughed. "I bet Teddy would be much better than me," said April. "By the way, where is he?"

"Your mother and I have arranged for him to arrive in about a week or so," Hermes told the young girl. "Have there been any further objections from his parents, Rowena?"

"Nope," she told him. Rowena had recently been keeping in touch with Mr. and Mrs. Evans after Teddy had given Hermes his parents' numbers through a series of passed notes to Watt and Fade. Hermes had given these numbers to Rowena when she first arrived at his cave. She had introduced herself to Teddy's parents (who knew who she was from Teddy's elaborate story), explained why she, Hermes, and the Sorcerer Council were trustworthy, and also given them a similar excuse that she had used (in her version, April got a deadly illness from the Alaskan environment and in the version she gave to the Evans family, Teddy and his cousins caught the disease from April). Since Mr. and Mrs. Evans shared this coverup story with the Robinsons and the Montys, a test had been done in Wisconsin trying to prove how the disease started and if it existed. Luckily, no one cared about the study, so the Montys, Robinsons, Evanses, and Finnegans avoided many lawsuits. Anyway, Rowena eventually managed to convince Teddy's parents that Hermes was a good person, magic was truly a natural phenomenon and not something created by evil dictators, and that Teddy should take sorcery lessons from Hermes. Finally, they had agreed to it under the condition that they came with Teddy when these lessons took place.

"Well, that's terrific news," said Hermes with a sigh of relief. "I had assumed that they would have figured out another way to object, but I suppose your extremely long conversations with them were enough. I am glad that they put up a bit of a fight, however; if they hadn't, I would question if they truly cared about Teddy."

"I agree," April responded and then looked at Rowena. "I used to think that maybe you were a bit too tough and over-protective, Mother, but then I realized just how dangerous the things we did were. I mean, most kids don't trek through the mountains to find their villainous uncles or fight their way through multiple countries to find out where their fathers are; I was just used to it."

"Oh, come on, it wasn't too dangerous," Rowena said some-what arrogantly. "But I would rather die myself than have a hair on your head harmed."

The two smiled at each other for a good long while in a bond only a parent and child can have, making it a somewhat awkward moment for Hermes. Luckily, two strange occurrences from outside of the cave allowed him to escape. "I think I might have a message," he told them. "I'll try to be right back, but if it is a particularly long one, remember to cast some more Oxygen and Heating Spells. This cave has a very high elevation, you know."

April and Rowena nodded and Hermes strolled to the mouth of the cave and scanned the sky and mountain rock for the strange occurrences he had caught a glimpse of. All of a sudden, paw prints appeared in the snow and Fade materialized with her feet in the tracks. The next thing Hermes knew, a lightning bolt struck the spot next to her and Watt appeared once it had faded away.

"Goodness!" he cried. "You mustn't scare me like that!" Then he laughed. "You must have some very serious news for me if it's that urgent."

He tapped his crystal to his head and a magenta ripple echoed through his body. Watt and Fade yipped and meowed loudly. As they did so, Hermes's eyebrows raised higher and higher, and the bags under his eyes seemed to grow deeper and deeper.

"No," he said, shaking his head. "You have heard wrong… this cannot be true. It cannot."

Tears appeared in Hermes's eyes. He turned around and ran back into the cave. Watt and Fade followed solemnly.

When the mother and daughter saw his state of distress, Rowena looked at him quizzically and April looked like a person awaiting the date of their execution.

"What's going on, Hermes?" Rowena asked him. "Why are you crying? Everything's fine!"

"Hermes, what news did Watt and Fade give you?" April asked worriedly. She then looked as if she was about to be sick, dreading whatever answer Hermes would possibly give.

The sorcerer closed his eyes, then inhaled and exhaled in order to stay calm. When he finally opened his eyes, the tears were gone but they were replaced by a look of pure horror and fear. He gulped, then finally spoke.

"The prophecy is coming true," he told them. "Lord Gregor Knotweigh is dead."